love wasted

SHIRL RICKMAN

Love Wasted \ Shirl Rickman – 1st ed.
Library of Congress Cataloging-in-Publication Data
ISBN-13: 978-0-692-90612-5

For lovers

love wasted

One

PAST

Cass: Age 12
Paxton: Age 14

Cass

"Jump Cass, jump!" Delaney shouts, her voice barely recognizable over the sounds of the waves crashing along the shoreline.

Wide-eyed, I shake my head from side to side, my heart racing. As I look up in the direction of where we both crawled our way down the cliffside, my breathing feels a little labored. I wipe my sweaty palms down the front of my shirt and when I glance back down at Delaney standing three feet below the ledge I'm standing on, I realize I didn't think this through so clearly. With my back pressed firmly against the wall of dirt and rock behind me, I don't even pay attention to the sharp point sticking into my shoulder blade. The ledge is smaller than I anticipated, the distance to the ground below farther. How many times have our

1

parents told us to stay off these paths? They warned us about the fact that these areas can give way at a moment's notice and now, as a lone tear drifts down my cheek, I wish I had listened.

"Seriously, Cass! It's not that far, and you won't be able to climb back up the way we came. You can't stay there forever. Jumping is your only option," Delaney insists. "I did it and look"—she holds her arms outstretched and spins in a circle— "I'm all right."

I know I don't have a choice, but I have a hard time imagining anything other than my twisted body lying on the hard sand beneath me.

Putting her hands on her hips, Delaney huffs out a breath. "Fine. I'm going to find Paxton. He'll help you down," she suggests as she spins on her heels.

I step forward without thinking, calling after her, "Laney, no!" My foot slips a little and I let out a scream, grasping for the wall behind me. It was a close call, but I remain on my feet and back up against the cliff once again. "Please don't. He'll know we followed him," I plead.

She rolls her eyes. "Who cares?" Her voice echoes around me, drowning out the seagulls flying above. "It's better than our parents finding out we came down here. If you don't jump by the count of five then I'm going to find him."

Delaney begins counting, cupping her hands around her mouth as she yells out as loud as she can, pausing a moment between each number. I can still barely hear her above the sounds of the ocean, but when she calls out four, I take a step forward again, closing my eyes. As five leaves her lips, I hesitate, open my eyes, and scream, although my body remains frozen on the narrow ledge.

Shaking her head, Delaney turns without another word. I want to shout out and plead with her to find another way, but I know she's right. Paxton is my only hope of getting down without getting into trouble.

Paxton Luke is Delaney's older brother and the boy I've loved since the first time I laid my eyes on him at the age of seven. Every time I'm around him, my heart flutters. Of course, he's not thrilled about having a couple of sixth graders following him all the time. He's not grown, or even much older than us, but as the coolest eighth grader around, he thinks he's far more mature than we are. I don't care that he hasn't noticed me. My boobs are starting to come in, and as reluctant as my mom was to allow me to wear a two-piece swimsuit, I'm beginning to fill it out, which is everything a fourteen-year-old boy like Paxton Luke notices— or so I think because he has seemed to enjoy watching Cara Halloway prance around in her bikini for the last two summers.

I want him to notice me.

See me.

I'm a young woman, not just his baby sister's best friend.

It's the reason I agreed to Delaney's plan of following the guys and hanging with the older kids on the beach tonight. I agreed because I'm positive he will notice me, will finally recognize that I'm not some silly little girl anymore. I wanted him to notice me, just not this way.

As soon as the thought passes through my mind, I hear Paxton's deepening voice. "Laney, what in the hell were you and Cassandra thinking?" My attention follows the sound, and I notice them hurriedly walking toward me down the beach with a group of his friends following closely behind.

"We were thinking a bonfire sounded fun," Delaney states defiantly.

"Dude, she looks scared," someone says from behind Paxton and Laney. That's the moment his eyes meet mine, and I see a flicker of tenderness flash in his gaze before he shakes it off.

He stands below me and the small ledge. Raising his arms in the air, he shouts, "Cassandra, I want you to jump to me, and I'll catch you!"

"You can't!" I yell back down to him.

"I can and I will! Now, dammit, just jump Cass!" he urges me.

I slowly move to the edge and stare down at him. I hesitate.

"On three," he says. "One…two…three!"

I do it. I fall forward, eyes closed, arms out, screaming. It's a relatively short drop and our chests thump against one another before I have time to even think about falling. Paxton tries to hold his balance, but it's hard with the momentum of my fall and the shifting sand below his feet.

When I open my eyes, we're face to face, my mouth inches away from his, and I lick my lips. I'm about to actually kiss Paxton Luke. My first kiss. My brain is obviously not functioning, and I see the moment he realizes exactly what I'm thinking of doing. He quickly pushes me off him and stands, causing my face to hit the sand, and tiny grains stick to my lips and face.

As I lift my head and look up at him, his eyes are wide with shock, a little angry and a lot of embarrassment filling them. Matt and Zack are laughing behind him, and all of them are staring at me.

"Dude! She was going to kiss you," one of them says—I'm not sure which one because I'm still staring at Paxton.

"What the hell Cassandra? This," he says, waving his hand between us. "This will never happen. You're just a kid."

At that moment, I decide I won't hold back any longer.

I push myself up and shout, "I am not a kid! I…I love you!"

His face turns a dark shade of pink, Matt and Zack laugh louder, and Delaney gasps from somewhere behind me.

Paxton takes a step away from me and starts laughing, even though his face doesn't look like he finds humor in this situation at all. "Cassandra, you're a little girl. I could never love you. You're too silly and childish." He turns and starts to walk away before he shouts over his shoulder, "Go home and play with your dolls or something."

It's like a punch in the gut. He called me a little girl. He called me *silly*. Paxton said he'd never love me. I know love. I want to fall in love.

I, Cassandra Porter, love love.

The punch he just delivered with his words is so hard, it knocks the love for Paxton Luke right out of me. My eyes narrow and I know in that very moment, I don't love Paxton after all.

I hate him.

Paxton

The look on her face when I called her a silly little girl causes my stomach to turn. It hurt her. I didn't mean to hurt her…well, actually, that isn't the truth. I knew what it would make her feel before I said it. I may have *meant* to do it, but I didn't *want* to hurt her. I'm not sure why I did it… okay, that's a lie too. I know why.

It's because I hated seeing her scared. That funny feeling in my gut took over when I saw her, a feeling I don't want to have because Cass is twelve and my sister's best friend, and I'm fourteen and in eighth grade. So, I said it, and I laughed in her face.

I'm such a jerk, but Matt and Zach were standing there and they heard her and laughed. I was right to think they'd give me crap over it. Plus, I have other plans. I'm getting out of this

town. I'm going to make something of myself. I have big
dreams. I want to be an architect and design buildings. I can't
think of anything I have wanted more since my grandfather gave
me a book about the greatest architectural designs in the world. I
was fascinated, and that's when I knew. He told me I could do
anything I want as long as I have focus and work hard. So, I need
to focus, and everything about Cass Porter makes my focus blur-
ry.

It's the reason I laughed at her confession of love and said
what I said to her. It's the reason she looked at me for one brief
second like she might cry, but then instead gave me a look I've
never seen from her.

I walked away feeling like I would live to regret being cru-
el.

Two

PRESENT

Paxton

I'm not sure how many times I knock on Delaney's door before I finally decide to push it open. It's obvious no one is going to hear me over the sound of the music blasting inside the apartment. After closing the door behind me, I turn and face the strangers scattered in groups around the room. Searching through each of them, I try to find anything resembling my sister's face.

When I called her today and let her know my flight was landing tonight, she begged me to show up for this party until I couldn't say anything other than yes. She didn't tell me what the party is for, only that she was having one.

The dark room makes it harder to see. Thankfully the twinkle lights strung around the space give off enough light that I can see faces. My eyes connect with a cute brunette who gives me a smile that would normally have me ending the night with her straddling me and riding me until we're both sated. Tonight isn't that kind of night, though. I smile back and keep moving through the room.

Suddenly the room erupts into a chorus of "Happy Birthday" and before I know it, Laney is walking toward me, cake in hand, singing at the top of her lungs with everyone else.

Just as she turns and sets the cake on a table, the song comes to an end: "Happy birthday dear Cassandra! Happy birthday to you!" At the same moment, a light blonde head leans forward and blows out the candles.

Cassandra. Cassandra Porter.

It's her birthday. I wonder why Delaney didn't tell me this is a birthday party for Cassandra. The last time I saw her—which was probably briefly ten years ago when I was home last—she was her typical self.

Confident.

Mouthy.

Opinionated.

Uncomfortably polite.

It was uncomfortable because it never seemed sincere when she spoke to me. She kept her distance, and when she was forced to talk to me, it was curt and without much emotion.

With everyone else though? She showered them with kindness, kindness that wasn't forced and wasn't uncomfortable. She loved them, and they loved her.

Once the candles are blown out and Cass is pulling them from the cake, Delaney looks up and sees me. "Pax! Oh my god!" she screeches, running toward me and throwing her arms around my neck. Without hesitation, my arms return her embrace. "I've missed you! You're a sight for sore eyes!" We pull apart, looking at one another and grinning.

When I pull her back against me into a hug, my gaze looks beyond her shoulder and lands on a surprised pair of ice blue eyes. My lips lift in both corners, but Cassandra's stay neutral until two girls throw their arms around her, wishing her a happy birthday.

As I watch her accept well wishes, I'm struck by how different she looks—different, yet the same. She was always beautiful with her long blonde hair, sun-kissed skin, and pink lips, but now she seems more…more…*damn*, I can't put my finger on it.

"I didn't think you'd show," Delaney says accusingly.

Letting her go, I back up, taking my eyes away from the woman standing a few feet behind her. "Well, you were wrong," I tease. "Although, you didn't say the party was for Cassandra."

Delaney places her hands on her hips and tilts her head to one side a little as a slightly crooked smile spreads on her face. "Why does it matter whose party it is, especially Cassandra? You've known her practically your entire life."

Allowing my eyes to drift over Delaney's shoulder once more, I notice Cassandra is no longer standing there. Turning my attention back to my sister, I answer her. "Yes, I'm aware of how long I've known Cassandra, and that's exactly why you should've told me. I could've stopped for a present on my way."

A boisterous laugh escapes Delaney's lips. "Oh, yeah, sure—because you and Cassandra are so close."

"What's that supposed to mean? You did invite me to her party."

"Seriously, Pax? It's not like there's no love lost between the two of you. Also, I asked you to come because I wanted to see you, not because of Cass's party."

There's nothing for me to say to that because it's probably true. I don't know when it happened, but after years of Cassandra and Delaney lurking in my shadow, always following me and my friends around like the annoying little girls they were, one day they seemed to lose interest.

The older we got, the less Cass spoke to me and the more she talked to everyone else. In fact, she was always in love with someone else. The last time I saw her was ten years ago, the only time I came home after I left for college at NYU. It was Christmas and because I tried to prove a point to her and to myself, things got awkward. We never had a chance to talk about it because she was gone again. I called her, wanting to explain, and I even tried getting to her through Delaney, but she refused. I haven't seen or talked to her since then.

"Yeah..." I turn and face the room around us. I spot the birthday girl once again, standing with a glass of champagne in her hand and staring out the window overlooking the city. Her beauty strikes me in a way it never has before. I've always known Cassandra was something to admire, but tonight, in this light, coupled with the fact that I haven't seen her in years, I'm noticing something different, something I still can't put my finger on. "Yeah, you're right," I say to Delaney, walking away from her without looking back.

I don't stop until I'm standing directly behind Cassandra, my lips pressed against her ear. I don't know why I do it—I know it won't be welcome—but I can't bring myself to care. She squirms a little, trying to turn around, but I don't let her move. "Happy birthday, Cassandra Porter," I whisper.

Her body stiffens. "Thank you, Paxton Luke, but what in the hell are you doing?" Her voice is strong, fearless, and utterly musical.

Turning her around to face me, I hold her arms loosely behind her back.

Putting a smile on my face, I tell her, "I just wanted to wish my little sister's best friend a happy birthday."

"Let me go," she says, calmly but sternly.

"Why don't you like me, Cassandra?" I ask her, but I continue before she can answer. "Better yet, when did you *stop* liking me?" I let go of her arms and take a small step back.

She reaches up, tosses her long blonde hair over her shoulder, and takes a step forward. She leans in and a tiny smile stretches across her face as she whispers, "It's not that I don't like you or that I stopped, it's just that I'm completely indifferent to you." I'm stunned by her words as she straightens, pats me on the shoulder, and walks away, leaving me staring at her, speechless.

I'm never speechless.

"Thanks again for the birthday wishes," she yells over her shoulder after a moment. A tinkling of laughter follows after her words.

Suddenly, Delaney is standing next to me. "What was that all about?"

Looking down at her, I shake my head. "I'm not positive, but I think Cassandra hates me."

I watch her the rest of the night, flitting around the room, smiling, laughing, and talking with every person in the room but me. In fact, I'm fairly sure she never even looks my direction again. Why? And why do I care so much?

Why am I even still here?

Searching the room, I finally spot Delaney in a corner with a guy I can only presume is her latest conquest. I'm certain she texted me three weeks ago about some guy name Leo, but she sent me a picture of her and Leo, and that isn't him. Taking one last swig from my beer bottle, I make my way across the room to my sister.

"Sorry to interrupt," I say as I step up behind her. "But I'm out. It's going to be a long drive to Mom and Dad's."

She swivels around with a grin on her face.

"Awe, Pax," she coos, reaching out awkwardly and patting the side of my face. "Why are you leaving so soooooonnn?" She drags out the last word drunkenly.

"It's a long drive to Mom and Dad's," I restate, pulling her into a hug. "Slow down, Laney," I whisper in her ear. She giggles. Pushing away from her, I look into her eyes and smile. "I'll call you tomorrow." I place a light kiss to her forward and turn to leave, glaring at the guy behind her, who is obviously sober enough to put some distance between himself and my sister.

My eyes immediately land on Cassandra, and to my surprise, for the first time since she walked away, she's looking back at me. My lips tip up in the corner and I raise my hand in a small wave goodbye. Her expression doesn't change. She doesn't wave back, only stares. Just as I decide I'll go up to her and find out what her deal is once and for all, a tall, blond-haired guy walks up behind her, slips his arm around her waist, and places his lips along the column of her slender neck. Rather than step away in shock, Cassandra tilts her head to allow him more access. Her eyes remain locked with mine until the guy kisses his way up her skin and whispers something in her ear, causing her to smile and turn around in his embrace.

What in the hell is she doing? I think about going up to her, just as I did to Delaney, to suggest she call it quits on the alcohol for the night, but then I remember she isn't my sister. She isn't even my friend.

She's my no one.

Three

PRESENT

Cass

From the moment my eyes locked onto his, my night altered completely. I was having fun, feeling good, feeling carefree, happy, and fulfilled—despite the fact that my mom called only an hour before the party began and kindly reminded me that I need to figure out some areas of my life, namely my situation with Richard. For some reason, Paxton Luke is a harsher reminder of that.

I watched as he hugged Laney, gazed at his youthful smile, his teasing dark green eyes. He looked the same, but there was something in the way he held himself that had me wondering how he has changed. I was glad for the distraction when Monica and Lauren interrupted my thoughts to wish me a happy birthday. It was the perfect opportunity to put some distance between me and this ghost from my past.

As I looked out over the city, I thought about the life I've made for myself, the life Laney and I worked hard to have here, making it through college with honors, saving money, and scraping by so we could buy our own apartments. I admired the way the lights of the city were shining across the bay. It wasn't lost on me how lucky I am to be where I am at my age, to have the life I'm living. I'm successful in every area of my life except one. I have the job I want. I live in one of the most beautiful cities in the country, close to my best friend. I have everything. I even have a—

Before I could analyze my life any further, his breath was against my skin and his voice was in my ear. Paxton didn't realize how close he came to becoming impotent—I wasn't the top student in my self-defense class for no reason. Instead, I let him hold me, touch me, tease me in the way he always has, in a way that affects me in a way I never revealed to him.

I wasn't going to let him ruin my birthday. I walked away and didn't speak to him the rest of the night.

That doesn't mean I didn't think about him. I still saw him lurking. I saw him watching me from across the room, watching me laugh and drink champagne with my friends. I felt him. I hate the effect he still has on me after all these years. Even though I write about young love in my books, no one really falls in love at seven years old.

Exhausted by the night and the effects of the significant amount of alcohol I've had, I look up and find him staring at me. The partygoers are dwindling and I assume Pax is leaving because he just lifted his hand in a tiny wave. Relief washes over me. I haven't been able to breathe easily all night, and I know once he's gone I will be able to exhale. I don't want to feel the things he makes me feel.

Just as that thought crosses my mind, Richard's hand slides around my middle, his lips touching the soft skin of my neck. I tilt my head to give him more access and at first, my eyes remain locked on Paxton's. I see a flicker of something, but it disappears before I can decipher it.

The kisses Richard is peppering up my neck tickle, and I'm unable to hold back my smile. He is an attentive and kind lover. He's been good for me. Is he the one? I don't know.

When I glance back in Paxton's direction, he's still watching.

"It's time for your birthday gift," Richard whispers once he reaches my ear.

I can't look at him any longer. I don't understand him, so I turn in Richard's embrace, hoping to forget he's even here.

Cupping my face, Richard captures my mouth with his. His kiss is full of want and need. I accept it, hoping to drown out the world around us, the world Paxton Luke decided to walk back into, the little world I've spent time building a wall around, pretending he no longer exists.

Richard deepens the kiss. *Paxton doesn't exist. He doesn't matter.*

I repeat this to myself, just like I have for the last ten years.

I fiddle with the bracelet Richard gave me after our heavy makeout session on the balcony. It's beautiful, and on any other night I would've given in to the lust and rewarded him for his kind gesture, but tonight hasn't been any other night.

God dammit. I wasn't supposed to feel this way tonight. I wasn't meant to feel this way ever again. When I look up, I notice Richard laughing with two of the partners in Delaney's marketing firm who he's met on several occasions. His laugh is what attracted me to him in the first place. It made me feel something in the pit of my stomach, created a happy and heady feeling inside of me.

I wanted him to laugh at something I said. I wanted to laugh with him. I wanted to fall in love with him, so I tried my hardest to do just that. He became my person, maybe a crutch, someone I love being around even if he doesn't make my stomach feel like it's full of butterflies every time he touches me. I entered into a comfortable and uncomplicated relationship with Richard, one that worked for us both. He doesn't want to be attached, he only asks for loyalty. It was something I could give and have on and off for years. It took us some time to figure it all out, but we did and it's worked for us, for the most part.

"You have that look again," Laney says from behind me. She puts her hand on my shoulder and gives me a nudge. "Why do you have that look, Cass? I thought you were happy. I thought things were right this time." She takes a seat across from me, resting her chin in her hands.

I try to ignore her comment. "You look drunk."

"Oh no you don't," Laney declares, waving her finger at me. I laugh. She's not drunk, but she's definitely feeling really good. "You have your look…*the* look, and I want to know why."

"What look?" I ask her, trying to avoid this conversation for as long as I can.

Delaney continues waving her finger from side to side, rolling her eyes at me. "No, no, no, little Dr. Lovegood, you know exactly what look I'm referring to!"

I stare at Delaney dead in the eye. She doesn't flinch. Why and how does she see things even when she is inebriated? It boggles my mind how she does it, but she has known me since we were seven years old. She knows my moods, how I work, and what my fears and wants are…at least most of them. The bottom line is I'm not getting out of this conversation unless there's a sudden earthquake. I hold my breath, bracing for my unspoken wish. Nothing.

Fine, Mother Nature, don't help me. See if I put all of these wine bottles in the recycling tonight.

I glance away from Delaney and toward Richard. He's still in the midst of a conversation with the same guys as before, but this time he notices me watching him. He lifts his hand in a wave and smiles brightly in my direction. I raise my hand slightly, waving back. Laney's right. I've been wondering why Richard and I keep this thing going between us when it's going nowhere. We're using one another to pass the time, but why? When I look at him now, I wish I could love him, but I can't, no matter how hard I've tried. I know why I've been doing it, but why is he? Is it really as simple as the fact that I don't ask questions or pressure him for anything more than what we have right now—an intimacy and friendship where we can fulfill our sexual needs with someone we can trust?

"God dammit, Cassandra," Delaney scolds. "You're about to do it again." She points her finger in my direction. "This. This is what I meant by the look on your face. It's so easy to read you. You are about to start questioning your whole messed-up relationship with Richard! If it's not you then it's him. Either you get weird or he acts like a dick. I can't keep up. Five years of this shit is exhausting. One of you just needs to figure out this doesn't work anymore. You want more and it's not with him. It never has been with him."

"No!" I shout, startling even myself. I allow my eyes to roam around us to see if anyone noticed my outburst then turn my attention back to Delaney. "No," I state more calmly and firmly.

She doesn't try to hide the fact that she doesn't believe me when she rolls her eyes.

"One day your eyes are going to stick in the back of your head," I tell her. She doesn't laugh. She only shakes her head from side to side in a silent scolding.

"I don't believe you, Cass, but I also won't push you. I'm just begging you to take your romantic writer's heart's advice and see the possibility of happiness with Richard you saw the night you met him, or don't. You deserve happiness, in whatever form you choose, but make it what you really want. I've watched you do this too many times." She stands, swaying a little, and then she's suddenly pointing at me again. "Don't even say a word. Don't use the fact that I'm tipsy as a way out of listening to what I just told you."

I can't help the bark of laughter that escapes me. God, I love her. I watch her sway in the direction of her bedroom before she swivels around to face me. "Oh, and happy twenty-sixth, Cass! I love you, always have and always will. Be happy." Grinning ear to ear, she swings back around and stumbles the rest of the way to her room.

Watching her, I smile, thinking about how much I adore her.

Delaney does know me, so is she right about this? Do I sabotage myself? If so, why? How can I be so in love with the idea of love but never seem to get it right? I know why, and maybe she sees it too and wants me to just admit to the reason myself. It's because I can't shake the feelings I've tried to pretend don't exist.

It was so much easier before tonight and before Paxton. He just opened the door and allowed doubt back into my life.

Four

PAST

Cass: Age 14
Paxton: Age 16

Cass

"So, what's a girl like you doing at a party like this?" Johnny Ryan asks, the quirk of his lips just as attractive when he isn't smiling at all. He is even better looking up close than the ninth grade girls locker room gives him credit for.

I feel a chill run up my spine. Johnny is a senior at our high school. He is captain of the soccer team and well known around town for his surfing skills. He's also known for his way with the girls of our school. He's handsome, and he knows it.

"A-A girl like me?" I stutter out.

He takes a step toward me, reaching for my hand. When he takes it, he rubs his thumb gently over the top of mine. I look down at our hands, a nervous sensation moving around in my stomach. I like the way he's holding my hand. I like the way it makes me feel—flattered, pretty.

"Yes, a sweet, smart, cute freshman," he says, his voice thick and husky. "You're Cassandra Porter, right?" Johnny continues. *He knows my name? Me? A freshman?*

I push a loose strand of hair behind my ear nervously.

"I…uh… Yes, and you're Johnny Ryan," I respond, still staring at our linked hands.

He laughs a low, throaty laugh, dipping his head, trying to look me in the eyes. He's good—really good. Johnny has my full attention—I mean, I'm a fifteen-year-old girl who is very interested in being swept off her feet.

"You know my name?" He feigns shock. Johnny has to know everyone knows who he is. "That's cool."

I can't keep the grin on my face from growing. "Yes, and you know mine," I reply, trying to sound confident. There's that laugh again—it does something to my teenage insides.

"I make a habit of knowing the name of a pretty girl," Johnny says. I think it's supposed to be a compliment, one that is meant to make me melt at his feet, and I almost do, even if my brain realizes he's full of crap. I smile.

"Would you like a drink?" he asks, just as I notice the one person I spend time avoiding. *Paxton.* Delaney promised me he wouldn't be at this party—it's the one reason we decided it was safe to come. For Delaney, she would avoid a lecture, and for me, I could avoid him.

He walks into the room and everyone notices. I watch as girls stop talking, following him with their eyes. None of them move, almost in a trance. The guys start calling his name and slapping him on the back. Paxton just grins, his eyes searching the room, never focusing on any one person.

"Earth to Cassandra." Johnny's voice pulls me from my thoughts and when I glance back at him, he is giving me that lip quirk again. "Drink?" he asks again.

"Sure," I say, peeking over his shoulder one more time. When I do, Paxton is standing with his back to me, next to the keg.

Johnny laces his fingers with mine and tugs me in that direction. All eyes are on us; there are girls with their mouths hanging open and jealousy written on their faces.

Pushing my shoulders back, I brace myself for a run-in with Paxton. It always starts and ends in the same way, and I'm positive this time won't be any different. When he turns around, his eyes immediately land on mine and Johnny's interlocked hands, and I know my assumption isn't wrong. Paxton's eyes flash to Johnny's face and he takes a step forward.

"Johnny," Paxton says loudly, a strange tone in his voice. His gaze moves to my face. "Cass, what's going on here?" I feel stunned, and Johnny's hand tightens around mine as if he's protecting me.

"Dude, Paxton…Cassandra and I are just getting a drink," Johnny answers before I can say a word.

"Cassandra? What are you doing here? Is Delaney here too?" Paxton asks, ignoring Johnny and focusing on me.

"Seriously, Paxton!" I exclaim, a little louder than I intend. I step around Johnny. "What is your problem? Yes, Laney is here, and like Johnny said, we're getting a drink."

His face turns a light shade of red and he hands his drink to Matt, one of the guys on the soccer team.

"The hell you are!" He reaches for my free hand, taking hold and pulling me to him. It takes both myself and Johnny off guard and I'm propelled forward into Paxton's chest. "We're finding Laney and I'm taking you both home!"

"Dude, what the fuck?" Johnny shouts, taking a step toward Paxton. Johnny is a year older than Paxton, and even if he is a little smaller, he isn't afraid to stand up to him. Paxton doesn't shy away from confrontation either.

"Look, Johnny, this isn't happening. Cassandra is my sister's best friend, and they're not old enough to be here"—he waves his free hand between us—"doing this with you...with us."

Before either of them can say anything more, I yank my arm from Paxton's grasp. My lip is trembling, but I straighten my posture. He looks at me and begins to say something I've heard a thousand times from him. I cut him off before he can speak.

"First, you're not my brother, and second, you can't tell me what to do! In fact, our parents know Laney and I are here, so butt out!" I snap in his face. I have to look up at him because his six-foot-three-inch frame towers over me, even though I'm tall myself. Poking him in the chest, I keep going. "Stop telling us what to do, Paxton. You don't have a say in what I do with my life. I'm no one to you."

His nostrils flare as he glares down into my eyes. I can see a raging battle in the depths of his gaze, and I wait for his final push. It doesn't come. We remain locked in this war while everyone else around us watches, wondering what our next move will be. The girls who were ogling him earlier are whispering to one another, and the guys look to be divided on what move they should make if Pax and Johnny get in a fight, but I won't let it get that far.

"How about that drink, Johnny?" I say, my eyes never leaving Paxton.

"Uh, yeah, sure," he responds, sounding unsure. I'm still not sure what just happened, but there is always some kind of fight when it comes to Paxton and me.

"Great," I say sweetly. Turning to face Johnny, I catch a glimpse of Paxton shaking his head as he grabs his drink from Matt and tosses it back.

When I notice him later, watching me from the corner of the room as I talk to Johnny, I'm overcome by a dull ache in the pit of my stomach. It's the same feeling he always leaves me with—a hollow pang of sadness deep inside.

Paxton

I spent most of the night watching her. Matt tried to get me to go outside with two sophomore girls who wanted to "talk" in the pool house, but I blew him off. I didn't talk to anyone unless they came to me.

I also lost track of how many beers I had after she walked away with him.

The worst part of this whole situation is I've seen Johnny do this before with an incoming freshman—more than once. He turns on his charms and uses his jock status and popularity to lure them in. Cass wants me to leave her alone? Fine, I will, but she can't stop me from watching his every move so I can make sure he doesn't try anything.

He's trying all right, Cass just hasn't needed me to rescue her.

Every time he rubs his fingertips across her shoulder, she causes his hand to fall off subtly by turning away from him and looking around the room. It's obvious she isn't really into it, yet she stands and flirts with him all night and he keeps on trying.

A slow smile crosses my face as it dawns on me: Johnny Ryan may have met his match in Cass Porter. This five-foot-nine-inch gorgeous freshman girl waltzed into her first high school party and gave the most popular senior in our school a dose of his own medicine.

Man, that girl…her confidence and fire would knock any guy off his feet. I almost pity Johnny, but then I remember he's the one she's standing with instead of me.

PRESENT

Paxton

When I open my eyes, light is shining through the wooden blinds of my old bedroom and I sigh. It's strange being back here. It's been years, and I've avoided it. I just wanted to make it on my own, be my own person, get away from the stigma of where I grew up.

My parents never understood why I wanted to get away. They hated that I went to NYU, and it only got worse when Delaney chose Stanford and opted to stay close. She had no problem visiting regularly or going home for the holidays, unlike me.

When I graduated and chose to take the architecture internship in London instead of San Francisco, my mom cried and asked why I didn't want to be with them. What she didn't understand—what none of them understood—is that none of my decisions had to do with them; they had to do with me. I didn't love them less. I didn't hate them. *Shit*, I loved them more than anything, but making my own place in the world always meant something to me. I've always wanted to walk my own path, live life according to my rules.

I wanted success and independence. I live my life to please me—it's who I am—and that's exactly what I did. I made choices that gave me the security I have today. I am all the things I've always believed were important to me. I'm successful and proud, and I'm finally at the top of my field. That's the reason I came home—I made it, and now I'm going to make it here.

There's a light knock on my door before it creaks open. "Paxton? Are you awake?" asks the calming voice of my mother. Alexis Luke is youthful, soft-spoken, and artsy. Her dark hair and bright eyes would never reveal the fact that she is a mother of two humans in their mid-twenties.

The bed dips as she sits beside me and smiles. "Are you going to sleep all day? Should we have planned your welcome home get-together for tomorrow night to give you a day of rest?"

I give her a sleepy grin and take her hand in mine, squeezing it lightly. "I'm a bit jetlagged I guess, not to mention I stopped at Delaney's for Cass's birthday party so I was a little late getting to bed. I think I was up almost twenty-four hours," I say just before releasing a yawn.

Mom grins wider. "So you stopped by your sister's? Did she happen to say what time she'll be here this evening?" My poor mother is always waiting for her children. Delaney can be just as bad as me sometimes. She tends to move to the beat of her own drum, much to my parents' chagrin.

Sitting up, I stretch my arms over my head. "Nope, she wasn't really in a state to be thinking about her plans for today, much less thinking period." I laugh as my mother rolls her eyes.

"I'm telling you, you'd think those girls would have settled down by now, but no. Delaney never has a serious boyfriend, and Cassandra can't decide about the one she's had on and off for years. They may both have successful careers, but they can't seem to move forward in any other areas of their lives. I worry about them," she says, shaking her head.

She has Delaney pinned, but her description has me wondering about the woman Cassandra Porter is now. "Oh come on, Mom. You're overreacting. What's the difference between myself and Laney and Cass? We're happy, successful, and living our lives the way we want. They were celebrating last night. I'm sure they'll both figure out their romantic lives when the time is right." I say the words without much conviction. Thinking about Cass and the fact that she's spent years with some guy has me feeling something I've always avoided when it came to her. Sure, over the years while I've been away, my family has kept me up to date on all of the Porters' lives, but it's Cass's I paid most attention to when they told their stories. It has always been hard to keep things in check when it came to her. She was always a temptation.

She laughs and pats me on the shoulder as I sit up in bed. "I see some things never change." Her grin shines from ear to ear.

I rub my eyes and yawn again.

"What's that supposed to mean?" I ask her, stifling another yawn.

Standing, she makes her way to the doorway before turning back and looking at me, still grinning. "Your need to defend and protect those two, even from someone as harmless as your own mother," she clarifies. I stare up at her, feeling confused. "For the record, I'm glad you haven't changed. I've missed you. Hurry down—I know it's your party, but I need help with the desserts for tonight."

"Yeah, yeah, okay. I'll jump in the shower and be right down," I tell her as I get out of bed, an uneasy feeling filling my gut. I push it away because it doesn't make sense. I've been away a long time, and I shouldn't still feel this way when it comes to Cass—that conflicting feeling of want and guilt over allowing myself to want her. I push it aside.

"Thanks baby. Glad you're home," she says before leaving me alone once again.

Sighing, I look at the doorway my mom disappeared through. It does feel good to be home, familiar, safe. I'm just not sure I want everything to be the same anymore. I'm older, and I want different things. I need different things. I'm not the same.

After I step out of the shower, I quickly dry myself off, grab a pair of jeans and a hoodie from my suitcase, and get dressed.

When I walk into the kitchen, my dad is sitting at the table reading the paper. Our eyes meet, and a smile spreads across his face. Standing up, he walks over to me and wraps his arms around my shoulders. "Pax, your mother said you snuck in late last night."

Pulling out of the embrace, he sits back down while I pour myself a cup of coffee.

"Yeah, I stopped at Laney's last night for Cass's birthday party," I tell him, taking a sip of the hot liquid.

"Ah, yes. Delaney mentioned when we spoke a few days ago that they weren't driving down until today because she was throwing Cass a party. I'm glad she talked you into stopping by. She's missed you—we all have," he confides.

"Yeah, me too.

Where's Mom? She said she needed help with desserts," I say, moving to the fridge and opening it up. When I spot the half and half, I pull it off the top shelf and pour a little in my cup.

"She went to the store because she forgot something. Did your sister say what time she'd be here today?" Dad folds the paper before getting up and placing it in the recycle bin.

Taking another sip of my coffee, I walk over to the window, looking out at the ocean just beyond the cliff. "Nope. Like I told Mom, Laney was a bit too distracted to be thinking about what she was doing today, but I'd say it's safe to assume she won't be here before two," I joke.

My dad laughs with me. "Oh, to be young and single. It's all about the fun."

I look over at Dad like he has two heads. John Luke, like my mother, looks too young to have children in their twenties, but he has never been what people would call young at heart. His comment has me watching him closely, something I've never really done.

"Oh come on, Paxton, lighten up. I'm your dad, not a decrepit old man," he teases.

I explode in laughter. "Fine, not decrepit, but we may need to argue the whole *old* point."

"Har-har, kid! And you'll always be my kid, so don't try to argue that one," he tells me with a gleam of happiness in his eye.

Lifting my hands as if defending myself, I reply, "Whoa there, I wouldn't dare disagree with you on the morning of my return to the home clan." He laughs.

My dad pats me on the back as he walks past me. "I'm glad you're home, Pax. I've got to get the nice china out before your mom gets home—you know how she is about using her best dishes for the special occasions."

"Oh, I remember, and I'm happy to be home too, Dad. It's been too long," I confess.

He leaves me sitting alone, thinking about all the special occasions I've missed the last ten years—the family moments…all of the moments.

PRESENT

Cass

"Cassandra, I can't believe a girl who looks like you and writes such beautiful love stories hasn't found *the one* yet," my editor, Margo, exclaims over the phone. She called to let me know my latest manuscript is my best story to date.

I'm glad she can't see my face because I frown at her words.

Every time someone makes a comment like the one Margo just made to me, *fuck you* nearly slips from my mouth.

"I've met lots of men," I tell her smugly. "In fact, I've been dating Richard on a regular basis on and off for the last five years. We have a sort-of commitment." I grin as I think about Richard. He's romantic and charming, and *damn* he can kiss. He's also an asshole and selfish—can't have it all, I suppose.

"Richard, huh?" I hear Margo's voice echo. "And, tell me, when are the two of you finally going to actually commit?"

Rolling my eyes, I flop back on my bed. "It's…It's nice, but I don't know. He seems to care about me, and I love the way he kisses. He's been there for so long, and he's comfortable—we're comfortable. We trust each other."

Margo sighs. "See? This is what I mean, you…well, you write beautiful romance, but you can't seem to make it work for you in the real world." I can hear her rolling her eyes. "If I didn't read your love stories for a living, I wouldn't believe there was a romantic bone in your body," she adds.

"Now you're just being mean," I retort, a little peeved at the eternal judgment I receive from my so-called friends. "I'll have the final draft to you by next week. Goodbye Margo, and happy Sunday." I hang up the phone without even waiting to hear her farewell.

Standing abruptly, I stomp over to my closet and pull the door open.

Speaking of Richard, I was supposed to call him when I got up this morning, I just wasn't sure what I would say. After my conversation with Laney last night, I'm trying to keep my mind focused, open…open to the possibility of what I once saw in him, the possibility of us, which seemed to be on track until last night. I even thought about inviting him to Paxton's welcome home party at the Lukes', but it just doesn't feel right, especially now, in the midst of another one of our *what's happening between us* periods.

Plus, the memory of last night makes me want to drink, and it has nothing to do with turning a year older and everything to do with Paxton himself. It was the strangest encounter we've ever had, awkward and…something else. It's like he never left and the push and pull between us never stopped.

As I pull on my jeans and new soft blue cashmere sweater, I start humming the tune to Taylor Swift's "I Knew You Were Trouble."

"You know you need to stop listening to her music," Laney says from the doorway of my bedroom, startling me in the process.

"Oh shit! Dammit, Laney!" Throwing my hand over my heart, I glare at my best friend. "You need to knock before entering someone's apartment," I rebuke, still trying to pull my sweater over my head.

She walks farther into the room, making herself comfortable on my bed, seemingly ignoring my comment.

"Cass, you're my best friend. I have a key to your apartment, and you have one to mine. We've barely spent more than a week or two apart since we were seven years old. You are not just someone, so knocking seems silly in this circumstance," she says matter-of-factly, trying to rationalize her action.

Turning to face her, I rest my hand on my hip, cocking it to one side.

"Seriously, you and your brother need to learn some boundaries. I can't comprehend where the two of you get your bossy and intruding ways because neither of your parents are that way at all," I say, continuing to admonish her.

Delaney sits on her knees, tilting her head to one side as she looks at me.

"Cassandra, what has gotten into you? Even more important, why are you bringing Pax into it?" she questions, sounding confused and intrigued at the same time. "Are you two seriously still annoying one another?" She sits back on her haunches. "Man, this is going to be an awkward party."

Rolling my eyes, I swivel away from her. Searching through my closet for an overnight bag, I try to think of the right way to answer her. I need to say the right thing or she will make more out of this than there is.

"I guess I'm dreading seeing my mother after our conversation last night before the party. She brought up my age and my love life. As for Paxton, he has nothing to do with it really; I'm only stating the facts of our friendship over the years and how both of you have an obsessive need to boss me around," I explain, tossing a pair of polka dot pajamas into my bag.

"Ignore your mom, like I do mine, and as for Paxton, well, he just got back. He hasn't intruded in our lives for years. We're older, and he doesn't have a leg to stand on when it comes to bossing us around." A light giggle escapes her. "Ignore him too, like I do and like we've always done. It shouldn't be too hard since the party is for him and will be filled with his friends. He won't even care that we're there."

She's right. *Ignore Paxton.* After throwing in the last item I need for an overnight stay, I run and jump on my best friend, giggling along with her. What would life be like without her? I would never want to find out.

She reaches over and slaps me on the ass.

"Let's get on the road, and you're driving this time," she tells me, hopping off the bed in the process. "Also, don't forget the Tim Tams! I need sugar and hangover food."

Shaking my head, I get up off the bed, picking my bag up as I leave my room. I'm not sure what this weekend will be like, but I'm a smart, twenty-six-year-old successful author. I'm fine. My life is fine, and my romantic life is fine, even if it is a bit more on the *in care* side than the *in love* side.

As I pull into my parents' driveway, I notice neither of them is home. I glance over at Laney's house next door and realize Mrs. Luke's car is also gone.

"Seriously! Where in the heck are my parents?" I say out loud as I pull the keys from the ignition. Delaney is out of the car and opening the back door before I'm even out of my seat. "I'm going to throw a pretend temper tantrum over the fact that I can't open my birthday present until they get home." I grin over the top of the car at Laney and she rolls her eyes as usual.

"Who knows? It's the life of retirees, they get to do what they want. I don't think anyone is supposed to come over to my parents' house until six," she offers as she pulls her bag from the back. "You know how they are, Cass. Most likely, they're out buying last-minute groceries and presents for you, and probably for Pax too because they think they need to make up for the last ten years he's been gone."

Grabbing my bag from the back seat, I slam the door shut.

Now I'm the one rolling my eyes. "You're right, they're ridiculous when it comes to things like that. I'm exhausted, but I know we promised we'd help your mom with appetizers. Also, I promised Richard I would call this morning...I didn't call him, and he left a message some time when we were in the cell service vortex of Highway 1 between Half Moon Bay and Pescadero."

"Oh, Richard," she says in an accusing tone. "Let's get started on appetizers and then we might have time for a nap before the party."

"Sounds amazing, but what's with the tone?" I question as we walk around the hedges and through her parents' front yard.

Without looking at me, Laney responds, "What tone?" There's humor her voice now.

"The 'Oh, Richard' tone," I insist.

"Ah, that? Well, I may have been a bit tipsy last night, but I still recall our conversation," she reminds me.

"Let it go, Laney." I groan, thinking of the annoying conversation she pulled me into just as she pushes the front door open.

"Let what go?" says a familiar male voice just beyond Laney. *Great. What are the odds?* I guess pretty good since this is his parents' home. It's going to be really inconvenient having him back in California.

"Hey big brother! Cass wants me to let go of the fact that she's suddenly questioning her messed-up, so-called relationship with Richard for the millionth time," Laney reveals to Paxton.

"Richard? Is that the guy from last night?" he asks casually. I keep walking toward the stairs behind Laney, trying to remove myself from Paxton's company. "What, no hello, Cassandra?" There's sarcasm in his voice as he says my full name instead of the nickname everyone has called me my entire life.

"Hello, Paxton, and yes, Richard was the guy I was with at the party last night. He's the guy I've been dating for pretty much the last five years, and he isn't news," I say as my foot hits the first step. I don't know why I make it a point to say how long Richard and I have been doing whatever it is we're doing, but I do. I guess old habits die hard; I can't seem to help myself when it comes to trying to get some sort of reaction out of Paxton.

"Huh, well poor Dick," he says as if he feels sorry for him.

I stop on the step and partially turn toward Paxton. "It's Richard, and what does that mean?" I ask him in my usual talk-ing-to-Paxton tone. It's a *you're so irritating and why I do care what you think* tone I save especially for speaking to him and used practically our entire teen lives. I hate how he can make me revert to my immature ways so easily. I wait for him to answer.

"Just thinking about all the hearts you've broken over the years, and it sounds like he'll be joining the others in the broken hearts club," he jabs, looking like he's holding back laughter.

"Excuse me?" I growl, nearly jumping over the railing and strangling him to death. I feel Laney's hand suddenly take hold of my arm. *Why is he such an ass?*

"Pax, don't be a asshole. Forget I said anything, I was only teasing Cass. She and Richard are great. I mean, they have five years of...of whatever they call it between them, and it's their business. I just like harassing her," Laney says in my defense, pulling me up the stairs with her before I can say anything more.

"Chill out, I was only joking. Five years huh? I guess Cass stopped falling in and out of love like she changed clothes when we were growing up," Paxton says in a light tone, though his voice sounds a little strained.

"You can kiss my ass, Paxton Luke. It is good to see nothing has changed with you," I announce just as we disappear up the stairway.

Saying those words sends an aching feeling through me, and my heart feels like it might race out of my chest. My god, I wish one thing had changed—his effect on me.

Seven

PRESENT

Paxton

How'd I let my mom talk me into this? I don't really want the attention that comes along with a welcome home party. Hell, most of these people I haven't seen in years, and I don't really care to now. I would've liked a family get-together, but instead, I'm here with people I barely know anymore. The only person I kept in touch with on a regular basis aside from my family is Matt. I'd love it if I could just slide back into my life like I was never gone. I did it with my parents, with Laney. I tried with Cass, and maybe that's my clue that it's not possible.

She almost seems even more annoyed by me than when I left, which shouldn't be the case because our last night with each other was awkward to say the least.

Now, I'm standing in a room filled with a mix of my old friends and my parents' friends. At this moment, I'm listening to my best friend Matt regale a small group with the story of the time we decided to drive up to Waddell's at four in the morning to catch some waves. We were only sixteen at the time and didn't have our parents' permission. The two of us were always adventurous and caused a little innocent trouble for our parents. Of course, as things go when you're kids and doing things without permission, something always goes wrong—I broke my wrist in two places. Matt still has a way with stories and has everyone laughing at the image of me calling my parents from urgent care. Needless to say, they weren't happy. I laugh as my mom glares at me and my dad slaps me on the back.

Matt begins yet another story, and this time it's about Laney and Cass. As he begins entertaining the crowd with his animated reenactment, I eye the two stars of his story huddled in a corner with a bottle of champagne. Laney whispers in Cass's ear and she throws her head back in unbridled laughter.

What is it about her? From the moment her eyes met mine last night, I felt like the boy I was instead of the man I've become. I can't seem to help my reaction to her, but something is different. It's not the same now as it was before I left. There's a reason why seeing her, talking to her now isn't the same though —it's because I no longer feel as in control. There's something more to Cass than I remember, and I'm not sure I like the way it's making me feel.

Lost in my thoughts, I'm not even aware she's stopped laughing and is looking right at me until I look into her gaze.

Those eyes of hers remind me of all the times I didn't do anything but watch her. She'd pull me in without even realizing it. I'd fight the feelings she stirred in me any time I got caught up in her, and I would always make sure she knew it was nothing more than me teasing her. I would taunt her to prove to myself that I could, but the moment I felt too much, I'd push her away. Even if I wasn't fair to her, I always acted like she meant nothing. I'm not sure why I did it, but she was always a challenge. I always tested the waters between us, and I know that's the reason she hates me—because I made her feel like she meant nothing. It was a lie, but I had a dream and it didn't involve a relationship.

Apparently, she still has that effect on me, and the battle lines have been drawn once again.

Laney says something to her, drawing her attention back to my sister just about the time Matt asks me a question. When I turn back to the group, he repeats himself. "Why'd you stay away so long?" It's my least favorite question.

At the same moment, Laney and Cass walk up and join the small group.

I rub my hand over my head and down the back of my neck then squeeze, trying to ease the tension the question causes. "Well, my career. I was a workaholic, moving up the ladder. It just took up so much of my time, not to mention that my parents made it easy for me to stay away since they'd come visit often."

"So what made you come home?" Cass blurts out, surprising me. By the look on her face, she didn't mean to ask that out loud.

The corner of my mouth tilts up because as usual, she showed more interest than she intended. *Nope, sorry, there's no taking it back now, Cassandra.*

Pretending we're the only two people in the room, I look directly at her. "It was time. There's a lot I missed here…a lot of people I missed." She glares. I laugh. Everyone just watches us.

Laney punches me. "You're such a dumbass—you don't care about anyone or anything more than your job." Her statement stings, and I'm shocked by just how much. "If they hadn't offered you an opportunity you couldn't resist, you wouldn't be here now," she divulges to everyone.

"I guess things don't change." Matt laughs. "Same Paxton, everyone falling over themselves to have him, but the only thing he can see is his success." Now everyone laughs—everyone but me. When I look over at Cass, she isn't laughing either.

She excuses herself and walks down the hallway leading to the back door. I consider following her. It's instinctual, something I would've done in the past to make sure she was all right, but tonight, I think better of it. She doesn't want me, and she really isn't even my friend, she's Laney's, but damn if I don't feel responsible for the hurt I saw in her eyes when she walked away.

In the hour after Cass walks away, people begin saying their goodbyes and their many well wishes for my new job in the city. I decide to see if I can offer my mom any help cleaning up. When I walk into the kitchen, Cass is standing at the sink doing dishes while Laney dries them. Her hands are in the soapy water, and they're chatting in their usual easy manner.

Matt waltzes in behind me, picks up a dish towel, twists it up, and lets it fly, snapping it against Cass's arm. She swings around, screeching in the process. Laney joins her by glaring at Matt, too, while anticipating another assault by pointing a wooden spoon in his direction as defense.

"What the hell, Matt?" There is a fire in her eyes, and I can't decide if I want to punch Matt or laugh. Matt beams from ear to ear. He loves this stuff.

"Got ya, Cass the Sass!" He's laughing so hard. I haven't heard that nickname in years. It's like we're all teenagers again, back when Matt and I would give the girls a hard time. "Don't you even fucking think about it!" While I was lost in my short moment of nostalgia, Laney pulled out the sprayer from the sink and aimed it directly at Matt.

Laney quirks her brow and without another moment's hesitation, she squeezes the lever, spraying water all over the front of Matt's shirt. He charges her, and she keeps spraying. She's screaming, and he's yelling back. Cass is caught in the crossfire and jumps on Matt's back.

I can't control my laughter. I'm laughing so hard, I can barely breathe. Luckily, I am also smart enough to stay as far away as possible.

Suddenly, a loud booming voice sounds from behind me in a tone I haven't heard in years. "What in the hell is going on?" It's my dad, and although he's clearly annoyed, I can see his struggle to remain that way.

Soon Mom walks in behind him and says with a half-hysterical laugh, "What is wrong with you three? You're too old to be acting like a bunch of heathens!" The room goes silent.

That's all it takes. Laney, Cass, and Matt stop, look at one another, and then burst out laughing.

Mom and Dad look at the three idiots then my mom says, "You better clean this up, now. Cass, your mom and dad already went home and said they'd leave the door unlocked for you. We're going to bed. We're too old for late nights these days." You can hear a smile in her voice even as she and Dad shake their heads. Before they leave the room, Mom walks over to me and kisses my cheek, whispering, "Didn't you miss this?"

Once the laughter subsides, they all begin cleaning up the mess. It's like I'm not even here. I have the strangest feeling this isn't the first time this has happened, and it gives me an incredibly conflicted feeling.

I knew their lives went on without me, I just didn't expect to feel it. The three of them are obviously familiar with one another. They have their lives here, and they don't include me. Laney has her work, Matt has his business, and Cass has… I look at her more closely. She's smiling at something Matt says, and she's glowing. It seems Cass has moved on with her life the most. She has her writing career and that Richard guy.

Being home doesn't feel exactly like I hoped it would.

PRESENT

Cass

Every time I walk into my old bedroom in my parents' house, my instinct is to look out the window to the room across from mine, in the house next door—Paxton's room. Even when I knew he wasn't there, it was a hard habit to break.

Tonight though, for the first time in a long time, the light is on.

It's a strange feeling knowing he's back, just across the way. I hesitate to flip my light on so I can watch him. I stand in the darkness as his silhouette moves about his room, something I did many nights growing up. In a bizarre way, I realize now I kind of missed having him nearby.

Finally switching my light on, I close the door behind me and unzip my bag where it sits on the bed. I look around. Everything is exactly as it's been since my seventeenth birthday when my parents let me redecorate. The walls are a pale blue. Sheer white curtains that are just thick enough to block my room from view hang over the one window I was just looking out of. The quilt on my bed matches the walls perfectly.

As I pull out my pajamas, my phone starts ringing. When I pick it up, I see it's Richard's face lighting up the screen.

Tapping the connect button, I put the phone to my ear, walking around my bed to the opposite side so I can close the curtains before pulling my jeans off. "Hey, sorry I haven't had a chance to call you," I say immediately. "Laney and I helped her mom put some things together for the get-together then I took a nap as soon as we finished getting things ready. I was exhausted from last night. How was your day?"

I stick one foot then the other into my polka dot pajama shorts then pull one arm out of my top at a time while Richard tells me about his day. Moving the phone away from my ear and hitting the speakerphone button, I quickly throw on my navy tank.

Picking the phone back up, I take it off speaker. "Well, that sounds like a good day." I notice the light is off in Paxton's room, and for some reason, it makes me feel a little sad. "Uh…sorry, I'm just tired. Oh come on, Richard, don't be that way. Of course I had a fantastic time at my party last night, and I loved the bracelet." He sounds a little annoyed and keeps telling me I seem preoccupied. "My friend is home for the first time in ten years, give me a break…are you drunk?" I roll my eyes. He only acts irrational when he has been drinking, and it's also the only time he acts like he cares about what I'm doing when we're not together. "Look, let's talk tomorrow. I'm tired and want to go to bed. No, Richard…fine. Talk to you tomorrow. Good night." I hang up the phone, relieved to end that conversation. I have less and less patience with him lately. Laney's right—I'm definitely feeling like Richard and I are on different pages again.

Pulling the covers back, I start to slip into bed when I hear a knock, startling me. Then I hear my name coming from outside my window. Luckily, my parents now sleep with a white noise machine, so they sleep through anything. Where was that white noise machine during my teen years when I was trying to sneak in and out of the house?

I hear my name again with another soft knock.

I walk to the window, push back the light curtain, and bend to open the window. As I lean out, I come face to face with one Paxton Luke. "Pax?"

"Hey…uh…I'm sorry. I shouldn't have come over," he stutters out, appearing uncharacteristically nervous—his voice is normally full of confidence. I don't mean to smile, but I do. "You just smiled at me." His voice sounds triumphant. "Great, I can go now, because that's all I came over here for and you did it without any effort from me. Good night." There's laughter in his voice.

My heart goes pitter-pat at the sound of his deep, throaty laughter. I slap a hand against my chest right over the traitor and whisper, "Oh hell no you don't."

Paxton, of course, is still close enough to hear me. "No I don't, what?"

"Not you, my…never mind." Huffing out a sigh, I continue, "What did you really want, Paxton?"

He is silent a moment, moving closer to my window until we're face to face. "Why do you hate me?"

I can't do anything but stare at him. What the hell kind of question that? Why would he ask me that?

"Cass?" He actually sounds serious.

"It's not that I hate you, per se," I admit. "Kind of?"

"Huh, kind of?" he interrupts with a touch of sarcasm.

"I'm going to say this, and don't interrupt me, okay?"

Nodding, he doesn't say a word.

"I'm Laney's friend, and you're my best friend's brother, one I'm friendly with even though most of the time you don't deserve it. Trying to be your friend is one of the hardest damn things I've had to do. You're bossy and nosy and you love to get under my skin. We fight constantly because you can't seem to stop making it your mission to annoy me, and my hate for you…it's not hate. It's complicated."

He's so close, I can smell the minty scent of his toothpaste. His eyes never leave mine, and they look a little disappointed.

Finally, he speaks. "Don't ask me why I asked or why I act the way I do with you. I can't explain it. I'm not sure if I can or want to stop. It's our thing." He sighs. "I realized tonight that so much has changed, and I don't really like it. The only thing that hasn't changed is us—although, I did think you hated me."

"I do," I say without thinking. His eyebrows shoot up. "Well, I do. You infuriate me. You're arrogant and push me until I can't see straight. Like I said, it's complicated, but I think we could try to be friends…maybe."

Paxton slowly backs away and doesn't say anything. The silence becomes so awkward, the need to fill the quiet begs me to say something.

"What are you doing?"

"Night, Cass," he says before disappearing into the darkness that hangs between our houses.

"Good night, Paxton."

I still really want to hate you. Damn my heart.

Nine

PAST

Cass: Age 17
Paxton: Age 18 ½

Paxton

It's Christmas Eve, and I can smell my mom's sugar cookies wafting through the house. Our annual gathering with the Porters has started and I know my mom is going to be annoyed I'm not yet downstairs and participating in the festivities. I hear the timer go off, signaling that the cookies are about to come out of the oven, so I jump up to make a beeline for the hot, soft deliciousness.

When I come barreling down the hall and around the corner, I crash into Cassandra, who is standing in the entryway to the living room asking Laney if she needs more eggnog. *When did she get here?* That's a dumb question—she's always here, always in my peripheral vision where I can't ignore her.

As I bump into her, she lets out a tiny yelp and stumbles forward, but I instinctually grab her with my hands, pulling her into me—a little too close. I don't like being this close to Cass. She looks up at me, and for a moment I see something in her eyes other than her usual glare. It stirs something in me until I hear my sister say something causing some of their other friends in the room to giggle and Cassandra to huff out a breath of frustration.

"What?" I ask, looking over at my sister, confused.

The grin on her face grows wider before she says, "You're standing under the mistletoe holding Cass. The rule is you have to kiss." Her words are full of mischief and glee.

I stare at her like she's lost her mind until I feel Cassandra try to pull away. When I look back at her and into her crystal blue eyes, I see something unexpected: fear. For a split second, there's also unwanted desire. Hell, now I feel it, all of it. It's like all those emotions seeped right out of her and into me. She tries to pull away again.

"I don't think so," she announces shakily. "What is wrong with you, Laney? I'm not touching Paxton!" She says the words, but there's no conviction behind them.

I'm not sure what it is, but that does something to me. Her words feel like a challenge, and if there is one thing I never back down from, it's is a challenge. I tighten my grip. Cassandra's attention turns back to me, and I look directly into her eyes.

I find myself glancing down at her full, rosy lips then back up to her astonished gaze. I forget there are four other people in the room with us. I don't say anything out loud, but Cassandra reads my thoughts in my eyes. I know it the moment she realizes I'm going to kiss her.

"No, Pax. Don't," she begs in a quiet voice, her hands squeezing my arms, which are holding her against me.

I still don't say anything. I only shake my head, letting her know I deny her request. I'm going to kiss Cassandra Porter, right now, under the mistletoe.

I hover for a split second when our lips are mere inches apart as doubt tries to break through my desire to prove a point. I ignore that too, just like I ignore Cassandra's plea and the audience around us. I've made up my mind.

Lightly, I press my lips against her soft ones. Hers are tight at first, but I move to angle my mouth over hers and she softens. I pull her closer, and she comes willingly. A surge of lust suddenly burns up my body. This is a girl I swore I'd never kiss, and now I'm kissing her. We both pull away abruptly, eyes wide, and my lips are stinging with want.

Our gazes are locked in a battle of confusion and emotion, and then I see it. In the depth of her eyes, I see the hope, worry, and regret. She isn't happy about what just transpired between us. In fact, she hates me for it—I think she also hates herself.

"Whoa!" I hear Delaney exclaim from somewhere in the living room.

Now I feel confused and a little spiteful. The tiny spark of hope I see in her eyes makes me want to take control back because it forces me to feel anything but in control. I don't lose myself. I won't lose myself to lust or to love; it's weak.

Leaning forward, I press my mouth to her ear. She freezes at my nearness and I whisper, "I guess you finally got that kiss you always wanted." I don't know why I say it…I guess because I was beginning to feel the same kind of hope I saw in her eyes, and that can't happen. When I pull back, the look on her face has abruptly changed. One moment her face drains of all color, and then within seconds she recovers, full of fire.

"You don't know what I want," she spits out before shooting daggers at Delaney, who doesn't have a clue what she just started and is laughing uncontrollably on the couch while Cass storms away.

I'm an asshole, but I don't care. If I'm honest, I've thought about kissing Cass before, I just never went there. I've been gone at college for a few months, away from everything I know for the first time, and I've thought about her. Some things never change, and yet some things are different. Most things aren't. Either way, it doesn't matter. I have my reasons for never going there.

Cassandra Porter is fire, and I'm too smart to get burned.

PRESENT

Paxton

It's Christmas Eve, a little over a month since I've been home, since Cass and I had the conversation about where we stand with one another through the window of her bedroom. It should've stopped me from even putting us in this position. I said things could be different. I said we could try to be friends. This little stunt will not help my cause, but I just can't bring myself to give a damn at this moment.

We've been here before, in this same position, the same look and the same unspoken challenge. The only difference is we aren't seventeen and almost nineteen any longer. We aren't young kids. We are two adults fighting the same war we seem to have been fighting for years, and this time we're alone in the room. Our families gather in the kitchen, laughing and chatting in celebration of the holiday as we've done for years.

Our gazes lift to the traditional greenish plant with white berries hanging above our head then back to one another. A shared memory is flashing between us with a simple look.

I wish I could remember the day the lines were drawn between Cassandra and me, putting us on different sides, because the gleam of loathing I see in her eyes seems to be preparing for war. My grip on her wrist tightens and she doesn't even try to pull away; she knows it's no use, but the look in her eyes sharpens. She's throwing down the gauntlet.

Oh, Cass, you really should stop with the silent dares. It only makes me want to win this game, the game we just can't seem to stop playing with one another, both of us dancing around the other, waiting for the other to make a move first but not understanding what kind of move to make, never making our move.

Never say never.

I breathe out her name. "Cassandra." She takes a step away from me, her back hitting the wall behind her. I stalk her, matching her steps, her eyes widening until I move my lips to hover just above hers. Then Cass's eyes close as if she might be surrendering. I whisper her name again, wanting her to open her eyes so I know she's present for this moment, but when her eyes flash open, I don't see what I hoped to see. I can't even explain why I'm doing this, but the moment presented itself and the memory of a shared kiss tempted me.

Her hand rises between us, rests on my chest, and gives me a little push.

"Not this time, Pax. I'm saying no, and I mean it. You don't get to do what you want because you want to feel like you're in charge. You've always controlled every situation when it comes to me, like you own me, but you don't always get to be in control. I won't let you. Why do you do this? I just don't get you," she states assertively.

Control her? Her perception of our relationship over the years is completely different than mine—rational thinking has always been a struggle for her. I wish I could control her in some ways. There's a part of me that would like to dictate how this situation will go right now and spank that tight little ass of hers until she begs me for more—but it's not the right time or the right place. Hell, it's not even the right person, but contrary to her belief, I've never felt in control of much when I'm around Cassandra Porter. It's the reason I've kept my distance. I've wanted one thing for as long as I could remember—to be an architect. It's something I knew the first time my dad bought me a book about architecture around the world. He thought I would like it because of my eight-year-old self's obsession with Legos and building things.

Then one day, I noticed her too. Her long blonde hair. Her pretty eyes and the vulnerable way she looked at me. I thought of her more than I thought about building things. It made me mad and I felt funny. I didn't like it so I vowed to stop. She wouldn't win.

Maybe that's the game. I've never let her get the best of me, and I'm not about to start now.

A quiet, harsh, devil-may-care laugh slips through my lips. I step toward her with my shoulders back and antagonizing mischief fueling my next words. "Cassandra Porter, if I wanted to control you, I would. Don't make the mistake of thinking otherwise."

With that, I leave her standing under the mistletoe, kissless and no doubt feeling downright indignant while I feel utterly bereft.

When I walk into the kitchen, laughter rings through the room. I instantly school my features, hiding my frustration, and put a smile on my face. Delaney turns at that moment and walks over, looping her arm with mine.

"Pax, please back me up and tell Dad we knew he was lying when he said Bambi went to a farm to run free and be happy. Tell him we are aware Bambi was hit by a car while we were at school," she demands, giggling.

Bambi was our annoying but cute little terrier when we were kids. She was run over by a car, and our dad tried to convince us it was unfair to keep her cooped up in the house all day and so she went to a farm with other dogs.

Smiling, I glance at our dad and shrug. "Sorry Pops, but we knew. I mean, let's face it, the cover story was awful. Laney and Cass cried for days and made me promise not to let you know we knew."

"What did I cry for days over?" Cass's voice echoes through the kitchen and Delaney smiles brightly at her friend. I don't turn around to watch her enter the room.

"My dad doesn't believe we knew he lied to us about sweet Bambi's fate," Delaney explains, glancing over to him and rolling her eyes. He folds his arms across his chest, giving her a look I assume is supposed to make her feel scolded, but he's failing completely.

"Oh, Mr. Luke, really?" Cass giggles while wrapping her arms around Delaney and squeezing. "We did cry for days. Laney and I annoyed Pax so badly, I think he wanted to strangle us."

"I didn't," I say so indignantly everyone turns to look at me, but the only gaze I return belongs to Cassandra. Her bright blue eyes connect with mine, daring me to explain why I suddenly changed the tone of the conversation with two simple words.

My mother pulls my attention to her when she clears her throat. "Honey, you were always either ready to kill these two or to kill someone else because of them. I wouldn't be surprised if their crying annoyed you. I know your patience with Laney often ran thin."

"Yeah, you were such a mean and bossy brother!" Delaney chimes in, winking at me as she speaks. I catch a glimpse of Cass's expression, one that makes it clear she agrees.

I laugh. "Well, you were such an annoying little brat," I respond. Everyone laughs, our parents' and Cass's heads nodding in agreement. I glance over to Cassandra again; she's beaming with happiness, looking lovingly at my sister. A burning sensation begins filling my chest, but I quickly push it away and turn my attention back to my parents. "So is it time for dessert yet?"

Mrs. Porter smiles, shaking her head. "Paxton Luke, I see your appetite hasn't changed a bit in the last ten years."

Mrs. Porter takes a pie from the refrigerator, grabs a knife, and begins slicing it. My dad and Mr. Porter grab the plates while my mom pulls forks from the drawer. Delaney and Cass give everyone a slice.

My family—my parents, Laney, even Mr. and Mrs. Porter and Cass—the people who were the happy constant in my childhood, they're the people I missed.

Everyone is chatting, smiling, and enjoying the tradition of being together. Time has passed—a lot of time—but as I look around the kitchen, it's like nothing has changed. Mom and Mrs. Porter talk to one another with fondness and familiarity. Dad and Mr. Porter are still happy to remain in the shadows, watching everyone. Delaney and Cass still whisper to one another while they stuff their faces with pie and whipped cream.

Cassandra.

Once again, she turns her gaze in my direction, and our eyes meet. What I see in them tells me not everything is the same. Some things have changed.

Eleven

PRESENT

Cass

I avoid him the rest of the evening, or maybe he avoids me. Either way, Paxton and I have very little interaction. We're cordial when necessary and share the occasional glance, but after his little game under the mistletoe, I haven't been able to relax. I escape to the corner of the family room, pretending to be working on my manuscript so no one will bother me.

If it weren't for our families and the fact that it's Christmas, I would leave.

What is his problem anyway? He's been torturing me since the moment he got home, antagonizing me as if we are still the same kids who lived next door to one another. Well, I have news for him: I'm not that girl anymore. I can't be baited. I won't let him make me feel like a fool. I refuse to let him manipulate me in any way. I've spent years perfecting the ability to ignore Paxton Luke and all his charms.

"Okay, spill it—now." Laney's whispered demand startles me from my thoughts.

Breaking her ginger snap cookie in half, she offers some to me. When I look up at her, taking the cookie offering, I think about the fact that I wouldn't have survived all of these years without Laney. Sure, she's arrogant, and her filter has holes in it the size of the Grand Canyon, but she's also loyal and funny and kind. That same holey filter may have gotten her in trouble a few times too many, but it also means she tells you exactly what you need to hear when you refuse to see the truth. We've been best friends for nineteen years, and I wouldn't change a thing. I talk to her about everything—everything except Paxton. As much as I try to make that a smaller issue than it is, it's an enormous part of me.

We only spoke about it once. It was the day he humiliated me in front of Laney and his friends, the day I decided I hated him, the day he crushed me and all the hero worship I had for him. She asked me if it was true, if I loved him, and if that was the reason she and I were best friends. I explained that I had loved him before, but that our friendship had nothing to do with it. She never asked if I loved him again. Only once she asked me if I hated him. Of course, I said yes, and we laughed. It wasn't a lie; I did—I *do* hate him.

Taking a seat on the floor next to me, she pulls me toward her, wrapping her arm around my shoulder. It's almost motherly, which *almost* makes me laugh because Laney is anything but maternal, but she is capable of an immense amount of love she doesn't share with most people.

"Seriously, Cass, what's up with you?" Her voice is concerned. "Is Richard being an asshole again?"

Shaking my head, I sigh. "It's not Richard...not this time anyway." I try to add a bit of humor to my tone to lessen her worry. I can't tell her what's really on my mind. "I'm just a little overwhelmed by life right now. Margo is hounding me about this manuscript, my mom is hounding me about getting older, there's the apartment renovations, and, well, Richard is hot one minute and cold the next. You know us, we're never quite on the same page, but for some reason, we keep rereading our story, hoping that will change someday."

Laney squeezes then releases me. "I can call Margo and tell her to shove it because, without you, she's nothing. Your mom's a little scary, but I'll go up against her for you if I have to, and Richard..." Laney takes a small breath before continuing, "I'd say if you've outgrown the story then maybe it's time to pick up another book, but that's for you to decide."

I don't say anything, and she doesn't expect me to.

Except, tonight, I want to say more. Sure, everything I said a moment ago is the truth. I am worried about all of these things, but tonight, like many times during our friendship, I left out one thing. I never tell her about Paxton—my love, my hate, my exasperation with his presumptions about his role in my life, and most importantly, the attraction to him that has followed me through the years like a shadow.

If it were anyone else, I would've told her, but it's not someone else. It's Paxton.

My heart and mind feel heavy, but I try to lighten the mood. "You're a sorry excuse for a friend." I lean out of her embrace and look at her with a hard look. "You didn't even mention how you can help me with my apartment renovation situation."

"How dare you? I told you I saved a cardboard box for you to live in. Market Street Maurice said he'd share his corner, what more do you want?" We bust out laughing so loud our family members, including Paxton, turn and look in our direction.

Although it's not even that funny, I can't stop laughing— even when I realize Paxton is watching me with a smile on his face that would generally make me feel more than I want. Instead, I pretend he isn't here and laugh with my best friend. They all soon lose interest in our outburst and go back to their card game.

When our laughter finally subsides, Laney proposes a solution. "I know you said Richard offered to let you stay with him, but I hope you realize you can stay at my place."

Relief? Is that what I'm feeling? I knew I could stay with Laney if I really needed to, but hearing her say it kind of gives me the permission I think I needed. I'm not sure Richard was entirely thrilled with the prospect of us living together, even if it was only going to be for a month.

"Really?" I say, and Laney rolls her eyes. "Okay, but the idea of this would be more fun if you were actually going to be home."

An expression I rarely see on Laney's face—a mixture of fear and anger—appears briefly before she wipes it away. "Yeah, but instead I'll be thousands and thousands of miles away in our New York office, working on a deal that will change everything, the deal of a lifetime."

I raise my eyebrow. "Are you worried about something?" I question her.

Incredulously, she gasps. "Are you serious? No, no…I have this in the bag." She turns her head and begins scrolling through my open Word document.

Watching her, I debate pushing the subject, but know if she really needed to talk, she'd tell me.

"You realize if you read that, I'm going to have to kill you," I joke, lightly elbowing her in the side. She looks up and sticks her tongue out in my direction. "Laney?"

Smiling, she faces me again. "Yeah?"

"You know I love you, right?" Leaning forward, I hug her hard.

"Uh, Cass, your obsession with love is so gross." She laughs as she hugs me back.

I know she loves me. She's my safety net, and I'm hers. The Luke family is responsible for the best parts of my life.

Twelve

PAST

Cass: Age 15
Paxton: Age 17

Cass

I t's dark, and Laney left me out here all alone. It's easier for her to sneak back into her house through the front door because her parents' room is on the opposite side of the house, not to mention next to her bedroom.

I, on the other hand, could never sneak through the front door. Instead, I have to open my bedroom window and climb through it quietly.

As I tiptoe up to my room, it hits me that I'm not wearing the best clothes for climbing through a window. Looking down at my attire, I groan at the short, tight jean skirt, crop top, and flip flops—cute, but not conducive to my reentry into my sanctuary.

Slowly pushing the window up, I reach in and push the sheer curtain to the side.

I look around me quickly when I think I hear something, but it's so dark out I can't see anything. I just want to get into the house and in bed. Slipping off my flip flops, I bend down and pick them up, dropping them through the open window.

Okay, so now the hard part. My window isn't exactly what I would call low to the ground. *Shit.* I glance around me one more time. It's not as if anyone would be able to see me in this pitch black anyway, but I wanted to be sure regardless. I don't see anyone so I do the only thing I can think of: I lift my skirt up around my waist. Good thing it's dark because I'm now standing in between mine and Laney's house in my barely there top and a pair of lacy white panties.

Placing my hands on the ledge beneath my window, I put one leg up, and that's when I hear it—or rather, that's when I hear *him.* I'd recognize that laugh anywhere; I memorized it years ago. Once upon a time, I did everything in my power to be able to listen to that sound, to be the one who made him laugh.

Paxton.

"You know Cass, this might be a good time to put your leg down and cover up," he tells me with laughter in his voice.

Quickly putting both feet back on the ground, lowering my skirt, I swing around and scowl at him. He probably can't even see me, and that irritates me even more.

"What are you doing out here?" I ask him in annoyance. "And why were you looking at me?"

"First, I saw you sneak around here and thought you might need a boost through the window, and second, I'm an almost eighteen-year-old guy—lacy panties tend to stun me into stupidity. I did say something pretty much immediately…well, close enough to immediately."

My heart rate begins to speed up. He's so annoying, but I try to sound as calm and in control as possible. I fail. "P-Pretty much?" I stammer out.

I feel him take a step closer to me more than I actually see him move. Instinctually, I take a step back, not from fear of him, but rather fear of myself. He takes another step until I'm pressing my back against the wall of the house. My heart is pounding in my chest. It isn't supposed to be doing that when it comes to Paxton Luke. My heart and I made a pact on the beach that day five years ago, and it has made good on that promise until tonight.

Heart, you're a treacherous asshole.

"I hesitated a minute or two," Paxton murmurs, our faces inches apart.

I hate him.

"A minute or…two," I say, my voice barely audible.

"Cass, why do you keep repeating everything I say?" he asks, his voice sounding strange to my ears. He leans in a little more and I raise my hand, touching his chest lightly. He swallows noticeably.

Am I repeating after him? Ugh. Speak, Cassandra. Speak. Deep breath. Don't let him do this to you. You're smart. You're confident. You don't need his attention. You don't want it.

Straightening my shoulders, I push his chest a little harder this time. "Move, Paxton," I demand, still quietly, so I don't wake my parents. He takes hold of my wrist, firm but gentle at the same time.

"Cass…" he says breathily.

"Let go, Paxton, and move. Why do you always have to act like such a jackass?" I pull my hand away and he lets me.

Running a hand through his hair, he turns away from me.

"I don't know, Cass," he answers, sounding a bit defeated. It confuses me, and I feel my heart wanting to do that thing again.

"No!" I say a little too loudly. I slap my hand over my mouth.

"No what?" Paxton asks me through the darkness.

"Not you, my...never mind," I reply, lowering my voice once again. "I've got to get back inside before we wake my parents. They'll ground me for life...or at least until I'm eighteen." I turn for the window and look down at my skirt again. "Shit," I huff out.

Before I know what's happening, two large hands wrap around my waist and lift me until I'm sitting on the windowsill.

"There," he says, not even a little bit out of breath.

I stare down at him, in shock and a little awe. He is always such an annoyance and causing me so much frustration; I rarely see the moments he actually helps me, the moments he possibly sees me and not through me. I crawl the rest of the way through the window and turn, hanging out partway.

"Tha—" I begin to tell him, but Paxton interrupts me.

"You best get to bed before your parents wake up," he murmurs before leaning forward and pressing a brief kiss to my forehead...my forehead, like he's eighty and I'm his four-year-old granddaughter. *Dammit*, my heart. "Good night Cass," he says as he turns back to his house and climbs through his bedroom window. *So that's how he snuck up on me.*

"Good night Paxton," I finally say back, but I don't think he heard me.

I slide the window shut, crawl into bed, and pray my heart will get its act together and remember we hate Paxton Luke.

Thirteen

PRESENT

Paxton

Lightly kicking the door open after I unlock it, I drop my biggest bag in the entryway of Laney's apartment before turning back and grabbing my two smaller ones. It's a long drive between my parents and Laney's apartment in the city, and I'm exhausted. Yawning, I close the door behind me, deciding to put my bags in my room later. I want to grab a drink first.

I grab a glass from the cabinet then pull the filtered water pitcher from the fridge. Drinking the entire glass in one gulp, I turn around, taking in the room now that it's light outside and not filled with forty of her closest friends. When she said I could stay and she'd be out of town on a work trip for six weeks, I breathed a sigh of relief. It would be hell driving into the city every day for work if I stayed at my parents. Admiring the space, I know I'm going to be comfortable here.

I set the glass in the sink and decide to go ahead and grab my bags to start unpacking no matter how tired I feel. I have an early meeting and although I'm fortunate enough to roll out of bed and land in my office, I want to be able to relax tonight. Stepping around the bar of the open kitchen and into the foyer, I bend to grab my bags then hear the sound of running water.

Without picking my bag up, I turn and follow the sound into Laney's bedroom. It's now apparent to me that I heard water running because the shower is on. Confused, I walk quietly to the bathroom door and push it slowly open. The room is steaming up, but I can still make out a long, lean figure standing under the spray of the shower—*Cassandra*.

A slow smile creeps across my face. I should leave. She doesn't even know I'm here. It's not right, but damn I think I'm getting hard just watching the way she moves under the water even if I can't see a single part of her body clearly.

What in the hell is she doing here? Isn't her apartment just upstairs?

Also, is she singing Britney Spears?

Holding back my laughter, I take a step back because I know it isn't right for me to be standing here when Cassandra doesn't even know I'm in the apartment, let alone the room. Leaving the door slightly cracked, I sit in the overstuffed chair Laney has in the corner of her bedroom and wait for her to come out. After a couple more minutes, I hear the water shut off. Then, more quickly than I anticipated, Cassandra walks through the door into the bedroom, completely naked.

She screams bloody murder and drops to the floor on the other side of the bed. I stand up, stunned at first. Then, as if on autopilot, I rush toward her like she's just been attacked and needs to be rescued.

"Don't you dare, Paxton Luke!" she screeches, her finger pointing at me as her eyes peek over the side of the bed.

"I...I..." I'm not even sure what I'm trying to say because all I can think about is Cass's naked body—her toned, coppery, perfectly bare body. All the blood rushed to the deck below, and now I can't form any words.

"What in the hell is wrong with you? I'm naked! You saw me naked! Oh my god, you saw me without clothes on!" She squeals some more, sounding hysterical, still hiding behind the bed.

"Without clothes on does usually mean naked." Humor in uncomfortable situations tends to be a bad idea, but I can't seem to help myself.

She glares in my direction, and I honestly believe if she had a knife, she'd stab me, possibly repeatedly. I try to smooth things over.

"Shit, Cass! I didn't expect you to walk out here butt ass naked! Do you always just walk around without your clothes on?" Now I'm hollering at her, and I have no idea why. I don't think I can hear. Can that happen so quickly after the brain loses blood flow?

She pulls the towel from her head and wraps it around her tight little body.

"Are you kidding me?" She looks pissed. "You can't just sneak up on me like that! What are you doing here, anyway? Laney isn't here. She won't be home for over a month," she continues, the tone of her voice scolding.

"Whoa, whoa, now hold on a minute. I know Laney isn't here," I say, beginning to get irritated at her tone. I rest my hands on my hips and we both give one another a hard stare. She's always been so beautiful when she's angry, and now I'm thinking about the fact that I now know what she looks like under that towel. *Dear God, my balls hurt.* I need to go.

Simultaneously, we shout, "Why are you here?" Then, "Laney said I could stay here."

What the fuck? I'm going to kill Laney.

"What?" Cassandra asks incredulously.

"You heard me—I'm staying here for a while until I find a place," I tell Cass, still annoyed by her nasty tone.

"But I'm staying here while my apartment is being renovated." Her voice has taken on an almost fearful tone. "Dammit, Delaney, if you were here right now, I'd kill you."

I smile at her. She's always talked to herself when she gets nervous or mad. It's good to see that hasn't changed.

"You know she can't hear you, right?" My antagonizing comment is rewarded with a Cassandra Porter scowl, a look I've seen more times than I can count over the years.

She doesn't even dignify the remark with a response. She moves right over it and says, "What are we going to do?"

Shrugging, I walk to the hallway. "There are two rooms, Cass. I'll stay in the guest room, which is what I was planning on doing anyway. You stay in here. I think we're both adult enough to live under the same roof while I look for a place to live and Cass's apartment is renovated. Hell, we practically lived together most of our lives."

I stop in the doorway and make the mistake of turning back and looking at her—really looking at her. After the nakedness, I didn't quite focus my attention in her direction, and now I can confirm it was a good call. Cass's hair is hanging in wet waves over her shoulders. Her skin is still damp, and the curves of her round breasts are visible over the top of the towel she has wrapped around her fit frame. The fact that the towel isn't very big and hits mid-thigh on her long, toned legs only creates more of a strain in my pants. I quickly turn and step around the wall a bit so I'm partially hidden.

"Are you serious?" she asks, apparently reluctant.

"Am I what?" I ask, once again losing my train of thought.

She speaks slowly, saying one word at a time. "Are. You. Serious?"

Well, there's another thing that hasn't changed about Cass—the way she talks to me is still on point.

"Yes, I'm serious. It's no big deal." Cassandra releases a big sigh, causing her breasts to heave, exposing a little more of them above the towel. I swallow hard. "See ya, roomie." I smirk, turning before I reveal my true feelings about our little predicament.

Uncomfortable doesn't even begin to describe what I'm feeling right now. I'm so hard, it's nearly impossible to walk. I need to remove myself from such close proximity to Cass. What the hell was Laney thinking when she suggested each of us stay at her apartment?

Picking my bags up, I make my way to the room I'll be staying in.

As I pass through the living room, I can hear Cass moving around, slamming drawers and talking to herself. It brings a smile to my face, and I actually chuckle out loud. This is going to be fun, even if everything in me says it is a bad idea.

Tossing my belongings on the bed, I reach for the smallest one and retrieve my phone, tapping the troublemaker's number. As it begins ringing, I start pacing.

"Hey big brother!" Laney's voice echoes cheerfully through the phone. "What's up?"

Shaking my head, I can't decide if she knows the mess she's created or if she is still so self-absorbed and clueless.

"So, Laney, is there something you maybe forgot to mention? Information I may have thought relevant when accepting your invitation to stay at your place for a while?" I keep my voice even yet insinuating.

"Not that I…oh, Cass is calling me…oh, fuck!" It's like I can hear the light bulb flipping on in her mind.

"Yeah, *oh fuck* is right," I say with a sarcastic edge. "I'm pretty sure you should let that go to voicemail and then delete it because whatever she has to say won't be pleasant to the ears. Protect your ears and life, Laney, and definitely ignore Cass's call."

"Holy shit, I promise I didn't do it on purpose." I can hear the truth in her words. Being mad at her for very long never works; she can be so oblivious sometimes, and she just can't help herself. "But damn if I don't wish I could be a fly on the wall of my apartment for the next month or so," she states, and my level of annoyance reaches its max.

"Dammit, Laney, not cool. Not cool at all. You know how things are between Cass and me on a good day—what do you think they're going to be like on a daily basis?" I scold, running a hand through my hair.

I stand up and look at my reflection in the mirror hanging over the dresser, starting to really worry about how this is going to work. We both work from home. I have a hard time resisting the urge to aggravate her, and Cass has a hard time resisting the desire for me to get taken out by a bus.

In typical Delaney fashion, she accepts no responsibility for her self-absorbed choices. "Come on, Pax. It will be okay. You were like family once. I know you've been gone a while, but it's not like you two haven't practically lived under the same roof a huge part of your life." Although she's using the same so-called logic I used with Cass only ten minutes ago, I don't like it, mainly because we aren't like family...at all. I don't get hard-ons when I look at my family, and I definitely don't want to push them up against the wall and fuck them until they're screaming my name. I groan just thinking about it.

"Don't you dare huff at me!" Laney shouts through the phone. If she knew I wasn't even thinking about my frustration with her any longer, she wouldn't sound so indignant—she'd probably kick my ass, or at least try. "Seriously, Pax, I've been under a lot of pressure at work. It's been months since I offered you a place to stay. I didn't even remember when I made the same offer to Cass. It was an easy mistake. Is it really that big of a deal? I mean, it's Cass. You both know one another better than most people, and as much as you drive her insane, you guys can play nice…right?"

I want to yell at her and say no, it won't be okay, but then I would have to explain why. I'm not willing to do that, especially at this point, so instead, I say, "No, we don't really know one another that well anymore." Although that's true, I'm only feeling this way because the image of Cass naked is so fresh in my mind. *I can handle this situation. No problem. It'll be fine. It's just Cassandra.* "Fine, you're right. I just don't think it will be as easy to persuade Cass to reach that same conclusion," I concede reluctantly.

"Just don't be…you. Be someone who doesn't annoy her. Be…nice." She giggles.

"I'm not even going to dignify that with a response." Her laughter is louder now. "Bye Delaney. Be safe, and don't take any shit from the competition on this trip."

She stops laughing abruptly. "Not a chance, big brother. He has no idea what he's in for with this account. Anyway, I think I'll wait at least twenty-four hours for Cass to get used to the thought of living under the same roof as you before I take her call. Love you." She hangs up, and I laugh because she is smart to avoid her best friend, at least for the near future.

Now I need to figure out how I'm going to make this new living arrangement work..

Fourteen

PRESENT

Cass

"Laney, I'm calling to inform you that I'm putting a hex on you. I just removed hair from your brush and stuck it in this voodoo doll that is the spitting image of you and will commence sticking pins in it as soon as I hang up this phone. I plan on making this slow and painful. Remember you deserve it, and don't even pretend not to know why. You know!" I end the call and fall back onto the bed.

I wish I were serious about the hex thing. Laney does deserve it, but we both know I won't. For one thing, I've threatened this before when she pulls her self-absorbed bullshit. She just gets so involved in her own life, she doesn't think. Two, I love her despite this flaw. I mean, we all have flaws, it's just a shame Laney's impacts me more than it should.

Releasing a sigh, I cover my face with the pillow.

I'm not alone, and that thought is unsettling, but I can admit the idea is only bothersome because it's Paxton who is in this apartment with me. I thought I would have time to think. It's the reason I didn't stay with Richard—I wanted to be alone. I wanted to think about my relationship with Richard. I wanted to think about my writing and all the things I avoid. I wanted to embrace being twenty-six years old and being okay with where I'm at in my life. I just wanted to be.

I can't just be.

There is no way for me to do any of what I want with Paxton around. His reentrance into my life from afar muddled things enough, but now he's only fifty feet away from me. He saw me without clothes on. He saw me *naked*. When I walked out of the bathroom and found him lounging in that chair, waiting with his crooked, handsome, charming Paxton Luke smile, I couldn't think, and by God if I didn't want him to just take me right there against the wall. My body being exposed to his gaze was like being lit on fire, igniting a slow burn until I was completely inflamed.

He said it would be simple. Simple? How will this ever be simple for me? Even when he was on the opposite side of the world, the idea of Paxton has never been simple.

Shit. What's wrong with me? I will not let him get the better of me. If it's not a big deal to him, then it won't be a big deal to me. I spent practically my entire childhood keeping Paxton Luke at a distance, so doing it as an adult shouldn't be a problem. I can do this.

Sitting up, I hop off the bed and make my way to the kitchen. Before Paxton showed up, my plan was to have some dinner, stick a movie in, and have a little sake, and I'm not going to change my plan just because his arrival caused a ripple in it.

I pull out the leftover Japanese food from the fridge and stick it in the microwave then grab the chilled sake.

While the food heats up, I walk over to the coffee table, set the sake down, and grab the remote then click the TV on. Bringing up the on-demand movie selection, I begin searching through the romantic comedies. Quickly, I decide on *Letters to Juliet*. There's just something about that movie that makes me feel better; it makes me laugh and feel hopeful that real love exists.

The microwave signals that the food is ready just as Paxton walks into the room in a tight-fitting t-shirt and sweats hanging low on his hips. *Simple. This is simple.*

"Hey, what's for dinner?" he asks, like he belongs here and this is any other night in our lives. God, I hate how at ease he is.

Walking past him into the kitchen, I reply, "Well, I'm having leftover Japanese." When I look over at him, he's watching me with a small grin on his face. Rolling my eyes, I internally scold myself for having manners and feeling obligated to offer him some of my dinner. "There's plenty if you want some, and I even have some sake that I'll share, but I swear to God if you say one thing about my choice in movies, I'll make your life miserable for the next month." I must keep the upper hand in this friendly invitation.

Putting his hands up like I just pulled a gun on him, Paxton vows, "I wouldn't dream of saying a word. You won't even know I'm here, promise." There's laughter in his voice. I give him side eye while grinning because I'm not sure he's capable of flying low on my radar, and I'm not sure if that is his fault or mine. Damn him for being so cute.

"We'll see," I retort. He pulls some plates out of the cabinet while I take the food out of the microwave. Silently, we move around one another in the kitchen. I dish out food for both of us while he gets us utensils.

He sighs. "Let's not talk about this again, but I want to say sorry about our little encounter earlier. I'll stay out of your room and make sure you have privacy." I freeze when I feel him standing closer to me. I look up into his eyes, which are the color of the sky when a storm is rolling in—gray with flecks of a greenish color—and his expression is sincere. I don't know what he sees in my eyes. I look into his gaze, trying to read what it might be. "We can make this work."

Nodding, I turn back to the food and finish putting it on our plates. "Don't worry about it. We'll make it work." I pick up my plate and start to walk away. I can feel him watching me. "We used to be friends, right? How hard can it be, even if you do get under my skin with expertise?" I look back for one brief moment and smile at my joke. Paxton isn't smiling. He just picks up his plate and joins me in the living room.

We sit on opposite ends of the sofa from one another, and I click the movie on while he pours each of us a small ceramic cup of sake then hands one to me.

"Thanks." I touch it to my mouth and tilt it back. The burn in my throat feels good.

We eat in silence, watching the movie and eating our food. Every once in a while, he pours us a refill. It's sweet and surprisingly comfortable.

A little more than halfway through the movie, Paxton clears his throat. I look over at him and realize he's debating saying something. I want to laugh because I can tell either whatever he wants to say makes him uneasy or he's afraid I'm going to bite his head off for talking during the movie.

I decide to put him out of his misery. "Say whatever it is you want to say, Pax."

He turns and faces me, a serious look on his face. It's not an expression I'm used to seeing from Pax. Usually, he's being funny, sarcastic, and annoying, never serious.

"I was just thinking, do you think people can actually meet someone at a young age like this, fall in love, be separated, and then come together again?" His question shocks me. I even feel a slight stab of pain, but I'm not quite clear about what he means.

He must see the confusion on my face because he tries to explain. "What I mean is, can a love you find when you're young last a considerable span of time when you're separated and grow into different people? Do you believe that's possible?"

How in the hell am I supposed to keep this living situation simple when he asks shit like this? I should've chosen *Guardians of the Galaxy* when he decided to join me tonight. I also realize I'm going to answer him honestly.

Turning toward him and bringing my feet up onto the couch, movie forgotten, I take a minute to gather my thoughts. "Yeah, I think it's possible." I look at his face and acknowledge that the years have been kind to him. He's beginning to get small crinkles at the corners of his eyes, but I know it because everything is a joke. He's happy. Paxton tilts his head a little; his expression tells me he's trying to understand why I'm looking at him the way I am.

After a moment, I continue, "I think, for some people, it's absolutely possible." I pause, gathering my thoughts, willing my emotions not to get the best of me. "Then there are some people who fall in love with the idea of someone. Even if it feels like the most real thing in the world to them, it's never realized, and when that person comes back into their lives, everything has changed."

I'm so lost in the idea of what I'm saying, I don't notice I am on the verge of tears until Paxton says my name questioningly. "Cass?"

I look away and busy myself pouring one last shot of sake then letting it slide down my throat before I begin picking up our plates. I can feel his eyes on my every move, but Paxton doesn't say anything. For once, he doesn't push me. He lets it go, which I know goes completely against his nature where I'm concerned.

"I think I'm done for the night," I tell him without looking his way. "I'm tired and I have an early meeting with my editor."

I walk away toward the kitchen then stop without turning around. "Thanks, Pax, for the company." I don't say more, just continue to the kitchen, thinking to myself that he might be right—this isn't going to be so bad after all.

Tiny white lies, avoidance—these are the things that come along with trying to be friends with Paxton.

He doesn't move, just turns back to the movie. "Good night Cass. See you in the morning."

"Good night Pax," I whisper. It's been a while, but tonight my mind will be busy reminding my heart we're not supposed to feel too much when it comes to Paxton Luke.

PRESENT

Paxton

Taking a sip from my coffee cup, I listen to one of the account mangers in the east coast office jabber on and on about our new project. I follow along on the PowerPoint set up on my computer, grateful they can't see me yawn every thirty seconds of this entirely-too-early-for-the-west-coast meeting.

Meetings like this won't happen often, and thank God for that because it's six in the morning. I'm exhausted, but when they do need me to be prepared and awake and direct questions my way, I can answer with efficiency. Normally, I would be well rested and wide awake, but after Cass went to bed last night, I couldn't sleep. I thought about her response to my question—can a person find love at a young age and it actually last? It ran through my mind over and over until my brain decided to switch to thinking about the change in her mood after she answered me.

Overall, this meeting is going better than expected.

Trying to keep my volume down so I don't wake Cass, I interrupt my coworker. "Excuse me, Tom. It's all well and good if we follow this timeline to perfection, which I'm confident we will. My only concern is we aren't the only ones with our hands in this and we've left no margin for error if someone doesn't keep pace with us. What is our plan to ensure we are prepared for this?" As Tom addresses my question, my attention is drawn to the near silent gait of someone behind me.

When I look over my shoulder, Cass freezes. Her tiny pajama shorts show entirely too much skin after our encounter yesterday. She gives me an apologetic smile—so damn cute. I wave her off with a smile of my own, trying my damnedest to pay attention to everything Tom is saying over the line since I'm the one who brought up this potential problem.

Once he finishes proposing a solution to our small issue, I respond, hoping we can finish this meeting. "Well, if we can make that work, I'd say we can expect the job to go well for us." I can hear Cass quietly moving around in the kitchen; it's distracting, yet comforting in a strange way. "Sounds good. Let's touch base in a week then again a week before we break ground." I pause as they all say their goodbyes. "Yes, thanks guys. We'll talk soon."

As I hang up the phone, Cass tiptoes past me and sits down, curling her feet under her in the overstuffed floral-print armchair next to me. I watch as she silently takes a sip, closing her eyes as it touches her lips. It's the most blissful look I've ever seen on her face. A small ache forms in my chest and I begin rubbing it away.

When her eyes open, she smiles sweetly. "Good morning. I hope it's okay if I sit here. I can always go stand in the kitchen and drink my coffee."

"Good morning, and no, it's fine. I'm done with my call."
My voice sounds a little foreign to my ears. I pick up my coffee
and take a drink. "Sorry if I woke you up."

"No, you didn't," she answers quickly. She smiles then continues a little more softly, "I have a conference call with my editor in half an hour so I set my alarm." Pointing at herself, she
adds, "This girl doesn't function without at least two cups of coffee to begin her day."

"Ah, I get that completely," I agree. "I still have a few calls
to make, but if I'm going to be in your way, I can always go in
my room. I get that you weren't expecting to have me around."
Setting my coffee down, I begin gathering my things.

Suddenly, Cass leans forward, her silky hand covering
mine, stopping me. "Pax, stop. It's fine. I'll go into my room for
my call, and then if you don't mind having me in the same room,
I'll sit at the table when I start going over my rewrites." I look
down at her hand resting on mine and she quickly pulls it away.

"Yeah…yeah, that's fine. We'll just work around one another," I agree.

"Good." She stands, heading in the direction of the kitchen.
Just before she reaches it, she turns back. "Oh and Pax, it's
strange hearing you sound so professional when I know what an
inappropriate jackass you can be." She giggles then disappears
into the kitchen.

"Ha-ha!" I call out after her, shaking my head with a huge
grin on my face.

Turning my attention back to the design plans for the new
building, I begin making notes on the various papers in front of
me.

I get a little lost in my work, and it feels good. I'm good—
no, I'm great at my job, and it's nice to feel in my element again
because I've felt a little lost since I moved back home. At some

point, I hear Cass on the phone in her room, but then I easily get caught back up in my own calls and work.

I'm not sure how much time has gone by when a plate of food suddenly appears in my view on the coffee table in front of me.

Looking up, my eyes land on the back of Cass as she walks away. "Hey, what's this?"

Twisting back around, she shrugs her shoulders. "I made some food and knew you couldn't possibly have eaten because you've been sitting there all morning. I thought you might be hungry. No biggie." When she starts to walk away I jump up and reach for arm, pull her around, and hug her.

She stiffens and then relaxes, her arms gradually returning my embrace.

"Thank you, Cass." When I release her, confusion and shock are written across her face.

"Uh, you're welcome." She tilts her head to the side like she's trying to work out a puzzle. "Really, Pax, it was nothing," Cass assures me.

Looking down into her eyes, I'm overcome with the urge to apologize. "I know, but I wanted to say thank you anyway." This feeling isn't something I've felt in a long time. I never apologize, because I do everything with purpose. "Cass, I understand this living situation isn't ideal. I get that we're trying to get to know one another again as friends, but there has been this wall between us for years, one I helped build. You always seem to pull me into this overwhelming need to push you because I can see you don't really like me." She begins to say something but I keep going. "Let me finish. I'm not sure when things changed between us. Sure, you are Laney's friend, but I always thought we were friends in a weird way too. So…shit, what I'm saying is I'm going to work hard on not being an asshole and trying to make sharing an apartment with me as easy as possible for you."

A small smile begins to spread slowly across her face.

"Damn Pax, I'm not sure I've ever heard you say so much at one time." A giggle escapes and it hits me right in the chest. "I think we can definitely work on being friends. I'm working hard on letting go of my past annoyances with you." She grins. "This situation isn't what you expected either, so don't worry about it. Things are going to be fine between us. Now eat, the food is actually a ploy to keep your mouth closed because I'm going to start working on my manuscript since my editor sent it back to me."

Now her grin covers her entire face and laughter dances in her clear blue eyes. It's contagious and before I know it, I'm smiling too.

"Fine, but I'll take care of dinner."

"Yes! My evil plan is a success. I was counting on you saying that because I don't think I'll be moving for a while."

Without another word, she saunters over to where she has her computer and notebooks all laid out on the table and gets to work.

My lips tip up at one corner. Yeah, this may not be so bad after all.

Sixteen

PRESENT

Cass

I haven't moved from my spot at the table in about five hours except for the two times I got up to use the bathroom. Paxton brought me a refill of coffee twice along with a couple of cans of sparkling water during that time. I requested a bag of trail mix, and he added that to the pile of papers without a single complaint. He basically waited on me all day. Sometimes he moved about the room on a conference call, and I occasionally found myself watching him.

Today isn't the first time I've compared the Paxton of today with the Paxton of ten years ago. He hasn't really changed much. I noticed the other night that the years have been kind to him, but there is something in him that's different. There have been a couple moments where he's acted just as he always did, but it's obvious it's not really who he is anymore. He's almost softer toward me in some ways.

But, as I've sat here today, I've mostly been working. It's been at least an hour since I've noticed Pax; I've been so lost in this chapter, trying to get it just right and make it flow with the rest of the story. I struggled a bit at first, but I think I finally got it.

Rubbing my eyes, I realize I need to stop for the night.

Suddenly, I'm aware of the smell of garlic and something else filling the air around me. My stomach growls loudly as I hit save on my document and shut my computer down. When I glance at my phone, I notice I've missed three calls from Richard throughout the day. Quickly tapping out a message, I apologize for missing his calls and let him know I've been super busy with edits and will call him tomorrow.

Setting my phone back down, I leave all of my stuff sitting on the table, stretch, and walk toward the bedroom. I can hear Paxton in the kitchen cooking, so I decide to take a quick shower and wash my face before the food is ready.

When I get into the room, I shut the door behind me, undress, and quickly shower. The hot water feels amazing on my aching shoulders, but I don't stay in very long. I get out and quickly change into comfortable clean clothes, and I feel so much better.

With one last check in the mirror, I wander back into the living room and find Paxton setting out dinner on the round coffee table.

"Hey," Pax greets me, smiling.

"Hey," I return, pulling my hair up and twisting it into a bun.

He continues moving around, arranging everything for us. "So, I made some pasta with sundried tomatoes, roasted garlic, and a little basil then baked some chicken breast. I wasn't sure what you'd want, but I distinctly remember you loving Italian night at my house so I figured pasta of any kind would be good."

Paxton walks back toward the kitchen, but before he disappears around the corner, he looks back at me. "Sit down and dig in, I forgot the wine glasses and bread."

When he comes back a few minutes later, I've already served both of us a helping and opened the bottle of pinot noir.

Neither of us says a word, and the silence is comfortable. When I take my first bite, I groan in delight. "Mmmmm, Pax, this is amazing. Thank you."

His face lights up in a pleased expression. "My pleasure. So how are the rewrites coming along?" he asks before taking his own bite. "Man, this *is* good."

I laugh. "Still cocky, I see. I guess that hasn't changed." We grin at one another while stuffing our faces full of pasta. When I finish chewing my bite, I take a sip of wine and answer his question. "They're going well. I got a lot done so thanks for the making sure I had food and liquids to make it through the day. It was nice...this is nice. What about you? The part of your day I heard sounds like you're working on a major project." Taking a huge bite of pasta, I almost laugh when his eyes go wide. "What? I like food," I announce proudly.

Shaking his head, he allows a quiet laugh to slip out. "I see that. As for work, yeah, a massive project. We're working on a building remodel in the Civic Center Historic District. There's a lot riding on it and I'm overseeing it. It means a lot to me because it's my baby, my first design I've done alone start to finish. It's everything I've worked for, Cass. It's pretty much the only thing I've ever wanted out of life for as long as I can remember. It feels good."

If there's one thing I know about Paxton Luke, it's that he has always been driven. He wanted to be an architect for as long as I can remember, and I haven't heard anything from Laney or our parents to indicate anything has changed. Paxton always made it clear it's the only thing he's always wanted from life, and he's doing it. I'm so happy for him, but I'd be a liar if I didn't admit that it hurts a little.

It's not like he would've ever chosen me, even if his work wasn't his whole world, but deep down I know it's why even as we got older, he never saw the possibility—not even the one time he came home for winter break and kissed me. We felt something, but then he said too much as usual. Of course, my absolute conviction of my hatred of him didn't give any clue that I might feel otherwise, but it wouldn't have mattered anyway at that point, and it seems his life focus hasn't changed.

"That's amazing, Pax. You deserve it. I know you've always wanted this. I can't remember a time you didn't talk about becoming a successful architect, and you've done it." I'm praising him, telling him not what I think he wants to hear, but the truth.

There's a shift between us. I'm not sure what it means or if he even notices it, but I do. I don't feel as angry, and it's the strangest feeling because I've spent so many years really angry.

I guess I don't completely hate Paxton Luke after all.

Seventeen

PAST

Cass: Age 16
Paxton: Age 18

Cass

Tommy Shepard has definitely improved his kissing skills since the first time we kissed in the eighth grade. My first kiss was a ploy to get Pax's attention, and you can guess how that turned out—complete failure. He didn't even notice.

Now, only two years later, I'm standing in my front yard just beyond a tree, finding out a kiss can feel like something special. Every sixteen-year-old girl wants to feel like her experience is distinct from any other.

Tommy's hand begins to move to the hem of my t-shirt, lifting it slowly, and my mind pauses a minute, questioning the decision to let him continue. Then he tilts his head just a little, making our lips seem so compatible that my head becomes foggy.

As his hand moves up the flat, smooth skin of my belly, I sigh, and that's when I'm startled by the booming voice of the one person I least expected at this moment.

"Cass, what the hell?"

Dropping my shirt immediately, Tommy quickly takes a step backward, stumbling away from me.

Eyes wide, I stare, shocked at an angry Paxton Luke. Tommy looks like he might be sick, his eyes never leaving Pax's stoic face.

"I…I…" *Shit. Get it together Cass.* I know Paxton feeds off of my lack of confidence. Squaring my shoulders, I clear my throat. "I feel like that should be my question to you. I'm on a date, and you're interrupting."

Pax's eyes narrow then his gaze bounces between Tommy and me. Tommy now looks like he's gone past the sick point and straight to the edge of death.

Stuttering, Tommy blurts out, "I didn't realize she was yours, Pax. I mean, I heard…well, never mind what I heard, but it was an accident."

"What?" Pax and I exclaim at the same time, both staring at Tommy incredulously.

"What have you heard?" Pax's face has changed from red to a sort of weird ashen color.

"I'm not his!" My voice is strangled. Those words never fail to sting a little.

"It's just… You know what, I gotta go. I'll miss curfew." Tommy practically sprints to his car without a glance back.

Without thinking, I swing and smack Pax on the arm. My hand stings a little.

"My turn—what the hell, Pax?" Angry, I continue, "You've got to stop scaring all the boys off!"

Rubbing his arm, he smirks. "You hit me."

"Don't you dare smile at me!" I scold him, but damn if I don't love that crooked smile.

"Look, Cass, Tommy Shepard is an asswipe. You don't need to be kissing him, let alone letting him feel you up. It would be all over the locker room," he lectures. Being lectured by Pax drives me insane.

"It's none of your business!" The volume of my voice rises as I speak.

I try stepping around him, but he wraps his hand around my arm, swinging me around.

"You are my business, Cass," he insists. I can't read the expression his face, but he looks like he's in pain. There's anger, and there's something else I can't put my finger on.

My heart resents him, hates him...*loves him.*

"No. I'm. Not. Stop this, Pax. Quit coming to my rescue when I don't ask for it—when I don't *need* it. Stop doing this to me. Why are you always butting in? What do you want?" The words spill from my mouth, words I shouldn't say, words I've always needed to say.

Releasing my arm, he takes a step away, turning toward his house. Staring after him, feeling a little defeated, I shake my head and turn for my own front door.

His voice freezes my retreat, but I don't turn around. "Because you're Laney's best friend and she cares about if you're hurt or not." He swallows before continuing, "I don't want anything from you."

Paxton

When I walk through the front door, I slam it behind me and walk past my very confused parents sitting in the living room.

"Hey Paxton, is everything okay? What's with slamming the door?" my dad asks.

With my head down, I continue toward the hallway. "Sorry. Everything is fine, I'm just tired. I'm going to bed."

I don't even wait for their response because my control is dwindling fast. I hear them both say, "Good night," in unison.

I push the door to my room open then close it, careful not to shut it with too much force.

I can't help it—my eyes lift to the window next to my desk that faces toward her bedroom. Her light is on and I can see her silhouette moving around behind the curtain. I walk over and yank my curtains closed then fall back onto my bed

"Dammit!" I let out a frustrated groan.

I lost my cool the moment I stepped out of my truck and saw that prick Tommy Shepard's hands on her. He was touching her soft skin, kissing her plump red lips. I wanted to rip his fucking head off. I almost did—then I remembered I don't do those things. I definitely don't get emotional over Cass.

I acted like an asshole and as usual, I hurt her.

Closing my eyes, I try to remind myself of all the reasons why I don't allow myself to give in. Losing it the way I did doesn't do anything but widen the distance between Cass and me, which might actually be for the best. It's definitely for the best. I'm about to leave for school anyway, and I need to stop hurting her. She needs to live her life because I sure as hell am going to live mine. Nothing will stand in my way.

I need to stay away from her because it isn't fair to either of us if I don't. When will I learn? Maybe I won't, or maybe one day I will. Maybe one day Cassandra Porter won't affect me the way she does now.

Maybe.

One day.

Eighteen

PRESENT

Cass

R ichard is here. This could go very badly…or this could be a good thing. I haven't exactly told him Paxton is living here with me. It's not that I'm hiding it from him, we just haven't spoken much and it hasn't come up. I need to tell him now though because Pax could be back at any minute.

When I open the door, he smiles and kisses me on the cheek. I invite him in and as he follows me into the apartment, he wraps his arms around my waist from behind, pulling me close.

"I've missed you." His husky voice flutters over the skin of my neck, causing goose bumps to pop up.

Turning in his arms, I look up at him and smile. "It's only been four days since I saw you, but there is something I need—" He pulls me against him, interrupting me by placing his lips over mine. One thing I've always loved about Richard is the way he kisses.

The kiss is warm and inviting, so very Richard, there's just one problem—something is off. It's reminiscent of the first days in our relationship. I enjoyed the way the kiss felt, but I couldn't seem to lose myself in it then…and now suddenly I can't all over again. My heart was confused before my birthday party, and now things are even more complicated.

"Cassandra." Richard says my name, walking me backward until my back touches the wall. His hand travels delicately over my skin and he nips at me just the way I like it, making me feel weak in the knees. He moves his mouth back over mine, deepening the kiss. My mind reminds me of our history; my body reminds me of the familiarity. Richard deserves for me to at least pay attention to what we have.

Wrapping my arms around his neck, I accept his kiss. As soon as I do, I hear the door slam behind us. We pull apart immediately, and I'm left staring at a stunned Paxton standing in the foyer.

"Who the hell are you?" I hear Richard demand then he glances my direction quickly before turning back to Paxton.

I have no words, especially when Paxton begins walking toward us. His eyes are trained on me until he is standing directly in front of us, and then they move to Richard. Sticking his hand out, Paxton greets him. "You must be Dick!" I cringe at the nickname because I know Richard hates it, not to mention there's a ring of sarcasm in Paxton's voice.

Richard takes his hand reluctantly and responds, "Richard…and you are?" My eyes are still bouncing between them.

"Paxton Luke, Laney's brother."

"And my current roommate!" I blurt out. They both look back in my direction like they're just remembering I'm here. Richard looks like he just took a blow to his pride, and Paxton's lips are turned up at both corners. I can read his eyes—he knows I'm uncomfortable, and he thrives on it.

"Well, that's my cue," Paxton announces, turning and heading toward his room. Just before he leaves the room, he turns back, grinning. "Oh, and pleased to meet you, Dick." Then he disappears through his door.

I can feel Richard's eyes boring down on me. Quickly, I face him. "I tried to tell you!"

"When?" He begins pacing, stopping with his hands on his hips as he waits for my answer. "Well?"

"Look, I did, or at least I was going to, but then we got a little sidetracked," I say, trying to explain. I reach out and place my hand on his arm. "It's Paxton. I've known him my whole life...he's like my..." I swallow hard because I'm about to say something that's never been true. "He's like my brother."

"He didn't look at you like a brother looks at a sister, Cassandra." His voice is hard.

Dropping my hand, I straighten my shoulders. "Are you kidding me? This isn't an issue; it's just temporary." My anger is rising because he is both wrong and right at that the same time and I know it. Nothing is ever black and white between Paxton and me, but that doesn't mean anything is going on. We got along for two days—barely; what's the big deal? I just don't want to explain myself to Richard about Paxton or anything to do with him.

"Is this why you didn't want to stay with me? Is something going—"

Pointing my finger at him, I shout, "Don't you dare finish that sentence!"

"What? I mean, he reappears in town and suddenly you start doing your Cass thing," he accuses.

"My Cass thing? Jesus, Richard, this is ridiculous." I'm getting angrier and angrier. "Paxton and our living arrangement have nothing to do with you and me. We've been doing this dance for years. Just last month you told me you weren't sure you'd ever be ready for a real commitment. We go through the same old thing all the time, dammit. Everything is fine—or at least I thought it was," I argue.

He walks over to me and pulls me into a hug.

"Not to mention, I'm on deadline, so if I've seemed distant, it's that and nothing else." I accept his embrace.

"I'm sorry. I just was surprised, that's all." I can tell he means it.

"Remember, we promised honesty will always come first," I remind him.

Richard kisses me, hard and demanding, like he's staking a claim, but it's brief. "I gotta go because I have an early flight, but I'll be back in time for New Year's Eve on Saturday. What time should I be here?"

We walk over to the door as I answer. "Let's say eight o'clock?"

"Sounds good." He leans forward and kisses me sweetly on my forehead.

"Be safe, and see you when you get back." I hug Richard and shut the door behind him.

When the door is closed, I lean my back against it and let out a long sigh. Everything feels wrong, even more so than it did a few weeks ago. Walking to the living room, I fall back onto the couch. I lie there a moment and listen carefully for any indication that Paxton is moving behind that wall.

I think about the look on his face—there was something in the way his eyes met mine, like he was asking me for something, but I don't know what it is. I'm a little torn. Richard believes me when I say this has nothing to do with Paxton...the problem is, I don't know if I believe me.

Nineteen

PRESENT

Paxton

I almost did something foolish. It felt like someone took a knife and gutted me when I walked in on Cass kissing that dipshit, Richard. I don't even know him, but I hate him already.

It started my first night back in town when I saw him pawing at her, but tonight it was worse. I hated the way he touched her. Kissed her. Looked at her. Talked to her. *Jesus, what is my problem?* I knew she was with him, and it's Cass—why does it even matter?

Picking up my phone, I tap the screen and wait for her to answer.

"Hello." Her voice echoes from the other end of the line. *Thank God.*

"Laney, tell me about this Richard guy."

"Pax, what in the hell are you talking about?" She sounds confused and distracted.

Feeling annoyed, I huff out, "Tell me about Richard. Tell me who, what, when, and especially, why Cass is with this guy."

She whispers to someone, her voice muffled, and then she speaks to me. "What is going on Pax? Why all the interest in Richard? I mean—oh my god, are you jealous?" There's a bit of shock and excitement in her voice.

"What? No! It's just…I want to know because I don't think I like him." I'm trying to explain myself to her but am failing miserably.

"Dude, you are acting weird, but here is what I will tell you: Richard is a guy—nice when he wants to be, but mostly an ass. For whatever reason, Cass has put up with his shit for the last five years, and he has put up with hers. It's been an on-and-off thing. As for why? That's not a question I can answer, so grow a pair and ask her yourself." She sighs. "God damn, this is weird. I'm hanging up now. Don't ever call me again. Mkay. Love you. Bye."

I hold my phone out and stare at it. She told me everything and nothing. What I heard is that Cass has history with this Richard guy, even if it has been inconsistent. *History...* Sitting on the side of the bed, I place my hands on my knees then lie back and stare at the ceiling.

The look on Cass's face when I walked in was guilty; I can't imagine what she saw on mine. It felt wrong seeing her kiss him, just like before, but tonight it physically hurt. Whatever it is I'm feeling, I can't do it. I don't want it.

I hear muffled voices coming from the living room and I can tell he's angry. It appears Cass didn't let him know I am staying here too; I wonder why. Squeezing my eyes shut, I remind myself that the why doesn't matter. This is Cass.

Their voices grow quiet, muffled, less angry sounding. I shouldn't be here. Why didn't I turn around as soon as I walked in? Because I am an arrogant asshole, that's why. I tried to make them uncomfortable. *Dammit.* She always does this to me.

Suddenly, I hear the door close. They must've left. *Thank God.* Now I can breathe again. I need to think about why I felt the way I did meeting him and how I'll deal with it the next time I see him, because there's no way in hell I'm going to be hiding out in my room every time he's over here.

After a few minutes, there's still no sign of them.

Deciding to head into the kitchen to make dinner, I get up and walk out of my room. As soon as I walk out, I see Cass, standing in front of the couch, facing me.

"Oh, I thought you and Dick left," I say nonchalantly, taking a jab in the process. I never said I was mature.

"Stop calling him that," she insists. "You're doing it on purpose to get under his skin—I just don't understand why when this is the first time you've actually met him."

Neither do I. "Why would I do that?" Now I'm acting like an asshole to her, and I can't even explain it.

She throws her hands in the air and starts to walk away. "Great, there's the Pax I know. I can't say I'm glad to see you again."

"Whoa, whoa, what the hell is that supposed to mean?" Her words rub me the wrong way. I position myself a few feet behind her.

Whipping around, she steps toward me, pointing her finger at my chest. "It means I was beginning to think you may have grown up at least a little. I decided to let go of how you acted that night at my birthday party then again at Christmas, but you just can't seem to let me be. It's like you're incapable of actually respecting me." She is breathing hard, full of frustration and disappointment, and a bit of sadness clouds her eyes.

"Give me a break!" I shout. I can't even explain why because I can see I'm hurting her and making things worse, which is what I want to do least in the world.

It's like I lit a short-fused bomb—she explodes. "Aaaa-ahhhhhh, you're such an asshole!" Her finger is now poking me in the chest, only annoying me more. The worst part is I don't even think any of what I'm feeling is directed at Cass. *Out of control* is all that comes to mind.

Grabbing her wrist to stop her, I yell back at her, "Cass! Stop it! I'm sorry."

"What is it? What? For some reason, I felt sorry for you having to see me kissing Richard, and I don't know why. Why should it matter?" Cass's voice starts to lose its fire and she relaxes her hand in mine.

Reaching a hand up, I place it on the side of her cheek, caressing it lightly. "I'm sorry. I don't know why I act like such an asshole sometimes." It's an apology, but it's a bit halfhearted.

"It felt like we came to a new understanding this week. Things have been good," she remarks.

Dropping my hand, I glance away before I reply, "I guess it bothered me a little, but he's your boyfriend and—"

"But he isn't," she states, talking over me.

My head swivels back in her direction. She's looking right at me, and now I'm confused. She can see it, and she sounds like she regrets saying those words.

"Richard and I are complicated. We're not exactly together, and we're not exactly apart," she confesses. "We have a history, and right now we're in an *on* period of our on-again, off-again relationship." Cass explaining this to me is worse than Laney's account of their relationship. It's quiet in the room around us and she takes my hand again. My chest burns. "Why would it bother you, Pax?"

I don't say anything, just allow my gaze to roam over her, hoping for the right words, hoping for some sort of justification for why seeing Cass with Richard felt wrong. Cass waits, her eyes begging me to find the right words too.

"You know what, let's just forget it. I was just a little taken off guard. It didn't bother me, I misspoke." Her eyes lose some of the light shining in them. "Let's not fight, Cass, okay?"

She peers at me beneath her lashes, her gaze never leaving my face.

"Yeah, sure…okay," she replies, her voice sounding unsure.

"I was just going to make dinner, want some?" I ask her, hoping we can just pretend this conversation never happened.

Shaking her head slowly, Cass takes a step back. "Thanks, but no. I think I'm going to just go to bed." Turning, she walks toward her room. "Good night, Pax."

"Uh, yeah, good night, Cass," I reply, a bit stunned and unsure of exactly where we stand now. It's always two steps forward, one step back with us.

I'd be lying if I said I didn't care, because damn if I don't feel like shit right now.

Twenty

PAST

Cass: Age 18
Paxton: Age 20

Paxton

When I step through the door of my apartment, I stagger over to the sofa, exhausted and slightly intoxicated. I snuck out of Bobby's party thirty minutes before the clock struck midnight. I whooped and hollered then say my goodbyes. It's an every year thing on New Year's because I don't do the kiss.

It's one of my rules to live by—never kiss at midnight because it never leads to anything good, and more often than not, it ends with expectations. I don't do expectations either.

Reaching for the remote, I push the power button and begin flipping through the channels. Before I know it, I've watched nearly the entire two hours of *When Harry Met Sally*. Laney loves this movie, and my friends would never let me live this down.

I glance over at the clock; it's getting close to midnight back home. I'm going to call her.

Searching around for my phone, I finally find it on the floor next to where I'm lying on the couch. I quickly tap my favorites and find Laney's number then hit the call button. It rings and rings and just when I'm about to hang up, a singsong voice flutters drunkenly into my ear.

"Laney's phone, Happy New Year!"

She sounds happy and bubbly. It's been a while since I've heard her voice, and she still sounds the same, which I guess is a dumb thing to think. I try to picture what she looked like when I left two years ago for school. With that nearly white-blonde hair hanging well past her shoulders in waves and an athletic, five-foot-nine-inch frame with tawny skin, she's hard to forget.

"Cass, is that you?" I ask, although, I know the answer to the question.

A giggle. "Who is this? Wait, don't tell me, let me guess. Say my name again."

I can't help smiling. "Cass."

There's silence on the other end of the line. "Oh, fuck." That word coming out of her mouth makes me laugh. "Paxton?" There's a certain reluctance in the way she says my name.

"The one and only," I tease. "Happy almost New Year, Cass."

A long pause. "Happy almost New Year, Pax." Her voice isn't quite as bubbly as it was when she answered the phone. "Let me find Laney, hold on."

I don't know why, but I stop her. For some reason, I want to talk to her more. I was missing home and thought I wanted to talk to Laney, but strangely, speaking to Cass instead feels exactly like what I need. I've missed her too…such a strange revelation, one I'm not going to explore.

"Wait, Cass," I say, my voice unusually desperate. "Tell me what's going on. What have you been up to?" Again, another long pause. More silence. "Cass? Are you still there?"

"Uh, yeah…yeah, I'm here." She pauses once more. "Not much, just school. Normal life of a college student, you know how it is." Her voice sounds a little less hesitant.

"That's great. What about Laney?" I still feel a little in a liquor fog.

"Let me get her and you can ask her yourself." Cass sounds a bit relieved at the prospect of getting off the phone with me.

"No, you know how Laney is, she won't tell me how she really is. You tell me." I feel a bit desperate to keep her on the phone.

"Uh, okay, well, Laney is Laney. You know her, always barely escaping trouble, testing the waters, but she always ends up on top." She laughs, letting her guard down a little more.

Laughing with her, I say, "Yeah, that sounds about right. You two were always walking a fine line."

"And you were always butting your nose into our business. It has been different without you here." Her words sound a bit sad.

"Yeah, it's definitely not the same now that I'm not chasing after you two. I've been in a lot fewer arguments over the last couple of years."

We continue to talk, taking turns catching the other up on our experiences at school. Cass tells me about our families' Christmas celebration. Then she tells me more stories I don't get from my phone calls with my parents or Laney. It makes me miss all of them even more, but my life is meant for more than staying where I was as who I was. I needed to leave home to find out if my dreams were attainable.

"This is nice," I tell her after a while.

"What's nice?" she asks, the sounds of chaos starting to grow louder somewhere near her.

Suddenly, I hear another voice yelling close to the phone. "Babe, it's almost midnight!" There's a rustling commotion through the phone.

"Cass?" I shout her name into the phone.

"Pax, I…" Her voice becomes muffled.

Three…two…one! I hear shouts of celebration through the phone.

"Cassandra, I want my kiss! Hang up the phone!" a male voice carries through the phone and I hear a giggle. Bubbly Cass is back—I'd recognize that laugh anywhere.

She's gone, and I hear the distinct sounds of two lips meeting.

"Happy New Year, Cass," I whisper into the phone, knowing she most likely can't hear me. I hang up and begin channel surfing again.

Twenty-One

PRESENT

Cass

Several questions are swirling through my mind at this hour of the night.

For example, when I try to stand, is this little paper toilet seat cover going to stick to my ass? Are my feet numb from the champagne or the magenta stilettoes I'm wearing? The most important question of the night is: why am I sitting in the bathroom stall of a bar, staring at the sticky, alcohol-laden floor? Not to mention the number one question I will never admit out loud: why can't I get the picture of the brunette that's been hanging on Paxton all night plunging to her death from a cliff out of my head?

Oh hell. I need to stop. There's only one person who can distract me from my dumb emotions—Laney.

Taking my phone from my clutch, I tap Laney's name under my favorites. When it begins to ring, I stand up, wobbling a little while shimmying my panties up my legs and pulling the bottom of my gold mini dress back down from around my waist. A giggle slips past my lips when I think of the hot mess I am tonight.

As Laney's voicemail echoes in my ear, I fall against the wall of the bathroom stall. "Dammit, Laney! I really wish you would've answered," I holler into the phone unnecessarily. I hear the sounds of feminine chatter drifting from two stalls down, likely girls making one last dash to the ladies' room before the countdown. I lower my voice, "Happy New Year. God, I wish you were here." I sigh. "You'd tell me like it is…you'd stop me from doing something stupid…but you're not here, and when I do that stupid thing, I'm going to blame you. Just a friendly warning." Pausing, I stare at the writing on the side of the stall and notice the use of the words *love* and *forever* written in twirly letters full of hope. I'm sure the voicemail is going to cut off any moment, so I say my goodbye. "Anyway, I love you, Laney, like whoa, and don't you forget it."

Ending the call, I glance at the time before opening my clutch and dropping my phone in. I have five minutes until midnight. Pushing the door open, I wobble my way out, slowly making my way to the sink. I wash my hands, drying them before I freshen up with a touch of hot pink lip gloss and a fluff of my hair. One final look, and I approve.

As I leave, three giggling girls walk into the bathroom. I recognize one of them as the girl who has repeatedly taken a nosedive off a cliff in my mind throughout the night—Paxton's conquest of the evening. She briefly makes eye contact with me and smiles. I hate her.

Realizing I should probably hurry and find Richard, I make my way down the dimly lit hallway, the noise from the crowded bar growing louder. I can hear the excitement spreading around the room. God, I hope Richard stayed where he said he'd be, and I hope Paxton has disappeared.

When I step around the corner, I look around the open room to see if I can spot Richard while thinking about another familiar face.

As the thought crosses my mind, I'm abruptly tugged into a dark corner before I can even register what's happening. The large hand wrapped around my wrist is slightly calloused. I recognize his smell and a tiny squeak slips out as I'm suddenly face to face with the one person I was trying to avoid.

"Dammit, Paxton! What the hell are you doing?" I shout, annoyance clear in my voice.

"Don't be mad, Cass. We've barely spoken tonight and I—" he starts, but I interrupt him before he can finish. Paxton finishing that statement isn't a good idea; I can feel it even in my bubbly champagne haze. He's intoxicated too, and we've played this game too many times. There's never a winner.

In the commotion around us, the countdown to midnight begins.

Ten...

My eyes widen when his grip tightens on my wrist.

Nine...

"Cass..." My name is barely audible when it leaves his mouth like he's taking his last breath.

Eight...

"Pax..." His name leaves me in the same desperate manner.

Seven...

Whatever this is passing between us, it's not right. This isn't us. We aren't an *us*.

Six...

Tugging me forward, our eyes still locked, his other hand slips around my waist and rests on my lower back.

Five...

The world around us continues to move, but I feel stuck in time, the girl who was once in love with a boy.

Four...

My focus drops to his mouth. His lips still draw me in with their pouty softness, almost too gentle for a guy, but sexy as hell.

Three...

Paxton.

Two...

All of a sudden, the mouth I've been admiring is hovering over mine, waiting, wanting approval. The tiny distance between us is electrifying. It doesn't matter. *Stop...no...*

One...

My name slips through his lips on a sigh, and it's like an alarm sounding off in my brain. The New Year rings and Paxton leans in to seal the start of the year at the same time I take a step back, pulling away in the process.

He reaches for me. My lips tingle, feeling like I've been kissed. Paxton's eyes are wide with disappointment, his mouth open slightly like he's about to say something.

I shake my head, silent amidst the chaos all around me.

I turn on my heel and push my way through the crowd without looking back, wiping away any memory of the look on Paxton's face the moment I walk away from him.

Looking forward, my gaze finally lands on Richard. He's laughing and whistling along with everyone around him. He's handsome, a different kind of familiar. Without another thought of what almost transpired seconds ago, I throw my arms around his neck, smashing my lips against his, taking him by surprise with a kiss that isn't his. It only takes a moment for him to reciprocate. When he pulls away and looks down into my eyes, a grin spreads across his face. "Happy New Year!" He yells above the crowd then pulls me into a tight hug.

Feeling overwhelmed by emotions, I try to keep him from seeing them written on my face. I don't need to see my expression to know I don't have the look of a girl who just kissed the man she loves on New Year's. My insides feel crushed, and I'm positive the ache I feel in my heart is written across my features. I'll hide in his embrace for another moment. No one has to see. I don't want anyone to see, especially Richard. Clenching my eyes shut, I allow myself to feel so I can let it go.

When Richard squeezes me tighter, I open my eyes again and rest my chin on his shoulder.

The light is bright and my vision is slightly blurred except for one person standing in the middle of the crowd, hands hanging at his side. The look on his face tells me he saw the kiss—his kiss—but how he really feels about it is indecipherable.

Twenty-Two

PRESENT

Paxton

This is not happening.

An emotion has crept in that I've never really given much thought to in all of my twenty-eight years. I may not have ever actually felt it, but I recognize it. I've seen it thousands of times in the eyes of my friends, girls I've been with, coworkers, even strangers, but never have I experienced it burning in me so brightly.

The red-hot ache hit me in the center of my chest the moment her lips touched his.

A midnight kiss that was supposed to be mine. A kiss I never thought meant so much. It's not like I've never pressed my mouth against Cass's or felt any kind of response to being near her. Only the strongest of men could not have a reaction to her strong, lean body, her drive, her talent. Something is different now. From the moment I saw her after first arriving home, I've wondered why I stayed away for nearly ten years. Thoughts of why I never claimed Cassandra as mine began haunting me. Now, only a couple weeks later, I'm watching her kiss him...again...except this time I'm starting to see things a bit differently.

I want Cassandra. I crave her more than I thought possible. She complicates what I've always thought I wanted for my life.

The kiss ends and he looks at her in a way that makes me want to punch a puppy. He pulls her against his body, turning a little in the process. I can see Cassandra's face now, peeking over his shoulder.

There's something not quite right about her expression. *Why, Cass? Why'd you walk away from me just a few moments ago?* Her eyes are closed, and I need her to open them. *Just open your eyes, Cassandra.* It's like she hears my plea because she's now looking directly at me.

There's pain clouding her usually bright cerulean eyes.

I want to hold her, take away the pain. Suddenly, it strikes me, the realization that I'm the one who's causing her pain. She's taken. Cass is not mine. The thought is like a punch in the gut.

Defeat—it's a strange feeling.

I'm responsible for stepping away from the possibility of Cass and me. She and I still live together temporarily.

We have nineteen years of friendship, and I have an obligation to that. I won't let us down. We're friends, and friends don't kiss the way I wanted to kiss Cassandra only moments ago. I decide I'll back off.

Taking a step back, I give her a slight nod then turn and walk through the crowd, away from her.

When I find Matt standing near the bar with the same group of girls from earlier, I become the Paxton Luke I've always been—the guy who doesn't wear his heart on his sleeve, the guy who doesn't feel jealousy, the guy who definitely doesn't lose himself over anyone, especially his little sister's best friend.

"Dude! Where have you been?" Matt shouts, slapping me on the shoulder. "Time for the first shots of the new year."

"Tequila," I tell him. Tequila seems like an excellent way to forget about the first five minutes of this year. "My treat."

"Hell yeah, man!" Matt grins, pulling the petite blonde he has in his arms closer, taking her mouth with his with an unbridled passion only someone intoxicated would display in a crowd. I turn away and signal the bartender.

"Five shots of tequila and a Jameson on the rocks," I yell so the brutish-looking bartender can hear me. He nods then begins filling the order. Turning, I lean against the bar and face the crowd. Matt is still mauling the blonde, and her friends are standing in a huddle laughing.

When the bartender lines our drinks up on the bar, I pay him then begin passing them out. The brunette who was hanging on my every word earlier brushes her fingertips against my hand and smiles. I smile back and clink my glass against hers. "To the new year and new friends," I bellow out, throwing the shot back then chasing it with a long swig of my whiskey. My throat burns, and I'll take that over the burning in my chest any day. I don't care what I drink as long as it takes away this pain I'm feeling.

Suddenly, I feel the warmth of someone pressing against me. When I turn, the brunette, whose name is Mandy—I think— is looking up at me with glassy eyes. My mind is a bit hazy too, trying to erase the memory of another girl. "So, I didn't get my New Year's kiss," she slurs slightly, giving me a dazzling smile.

"Oh yeah?" I respond, not caring what happens next.

"Yeah, and it doesn't appear you had yours either, or you wouldn't be standing here now. You'd be with the lucky girl who had the good fortune to be standing next to you at midnight." She steps closer, pressing her small, pert breasts firmly against my chest, sliding her hands up my chest and around my neck.

Throwing the last of the whiskey down my throat, I wrap my arms around her waist and pull her closer. I bend my head lower, toward her waiting mouth. My mind registers the fact that I don't need to bend to kiss Cassandra; she's the perfect height for me. I only have to move a little for our lips to connect. Amanda is different...*or is it Mandy? Same thing, right?* Her eyes are barely open, and mine are beginning to feel heavy.

"Well, I guess we better remedy our situation. We wouldn't want to be the only two people tonight without a New Year's kiss, now would we?" I don't wait for an answer, just touch my mouth to hers. She begins prodding my mouth open with her tongue and it feels wrong, but I block the thought from my mind and deepen the kiss, giving this girl what she wants. I shut off my brain, suppressing all thoughts and embracing the lust shooting down my spine. Lust—I know it, and I accept it. It's a familiar feeling and frankly, the only one I'm truly capable of. Lust is safe.

The kiss goes on and on. Soon our hands are involved and getting a little carried away for such a public setting, but I tell myself not to care. This is me. I don't even think about coming up for air until my mind faintly registers Matt's voice shouting the one name I'm trying to forget. "Cass the Sass! Where did you go? You missed Old Pax here buying our first round of shots in the new year! I think we need more!"

Slowly, I break up my make out session with...*Monica?* Lifting my head languidly, I focus my attention in the direction Matt is staring, pulling the brunette close to my side, casually leaving one arm around her shoulder.

Cassandra is standing stock-still, staring directly at me. Richard is at her side, accepting a shot from Matt.

I can see the hurt in her eyes, and there's also confusion and determination. She doesn't want to play this game either. The tiniest of sardonic smiles forms on her oval face, and I give her my own devil-may-care look.

Shaking her head, Cassandra faces Richard and Matt, accepting the tequila shot they are offering. She doesn't even wait for the group, just tosses it back and sucks the lime wedge they gave her with it. She slams it on the bar and signals the bartender for another.

Matt slams his back and high-fives her.

Richard wraps his arms around her middle, pulling her back against him and kissing her neck. My grip on this girl whose name I don't even know tightens and I watch as they all accept another shot from the bartender. Cassandra's tongue darts out, and everything in me tightens. *Fuck.* I need to leave.

"Sorry, Mmm…" I begin.

"Macy," she provides, a little saucily.

"Yeah, Macy, I'm going to call it a night. Uh, thanks…for the kiss and …thanks." I lean down and place a peck on her cheek—I don't want to be a complete dick. I can see the disappointment in her eyes, and even more when she glances in Cassandra's direction.

Clapping my hand on Matt's shoulder, I holler, "Dude, I'm outta here. Be safe and call for a ride."

"Nah, dude, you can't leave." He sounds disappointed.

My gaze lifts to find Cassandra watching me. "I'm done, done with tonight and done with this whole thing." My statement seems so simple, but it holds a lot of meaning. I mean it—I need to let go of whatever it is I'm feeling. Feelings are dangerous.

Reaching my hand out, I take Richard's hand. "Dick, good to see you again." He glares at me as I shake his hand. He has made it clear he doesn't like being called Dick, which has only prompted me to use the nickname more. I give him a knowing smile.

Leaning forward toward Cassandra, I make the second biggest mistake of the night: I place a soft, slightly lingering kiss on her forehead. It may have been brief and completely platonic, but the weight of it feels heavy. "Cass, see you in the morning at home." The look in her eyes gives nothing away.

I smile. She smiles. "Thanks, Pax. Happy New Year." We say more with our eyes—more lies.

It's all lies, but it's a deception I'm willing to embrace if it means I remain in control of myself.

Twenty-Three

PRESENT

Cass

There's a ringing in my head. It won't quit, and it feels like it's getting more persistent, louder. My head is throbbing. *So much pain—oh my god, do I have a tumor?* It's so dark. After a moment, the ringing stops. I try opening one eye, and the light streaming in through the blinds is like a lightning bolt to my head.

"Ahh," I moan. The ringing starts up again, and I realize it's my phone. Champagne is the devil. Reaching out toward the side table, I keep my eyes closed for fear I will be blinded by the sunlight coming into the room. *What the fuck, San Francisco? The one day you decide to let the sun shine without the cover of fog has to be the day I wake up in an ultimate vampire state?*

Without looking, I tap the screen just to make it stop ringing. "Hello," I groan. My mouth feels like someone shoved a million cotton balls into it.

"Hey Cass, Happy New Year!" Laney shouts, her words vibrating through my skull.

"Ssssshhhhh. Don't shout," I beg. "I think it's just nifty you've decided to stop ignoring me after a week on the one day my head feels like I was kicked between the eyes."

She giggles. "I wasn't ignoring you…well, maybe initially, but then work has just been nuts and with the time difference, it's made it too hard—not to mention, I was hoping if we didn't speak, my spiritual essence would disappear and your voodoo doll wouldn't work."

"Should I pull it out and see how it's working now?" I suggest without a hint of humor.

She laughs louder, causing me to hold my head. *I hate New Year's Eve.*

"I'm calling now, and that's all that matters. What stupid thing did you do or are you about to do?"

"Nothing," I state so quickly, even I can't deny I sound like a liar.

"Okay, you're the worst liar in the world, and you definitely can't lie to me—I know you too well," she informs me. "So what's up? Am I too late?" Her voice is only slightly serious. I can hear a bit of concern, although it's not Laney's thing to get too emotional.

Sighing, I whisper, "Yes and no—and yes."

"Cass…"

Interrupting, I sigh again. "Look, Laney, you know I've been all over the place with Richard." I start with that because my real problem will take a bit more guts to admit.

"Really? That's it, Richard again?" she remarks with an air of disappointment to her voice.

"Let me finish," I insist, trying to work up the nerve to continue. "It's not just Richard. Richard and I are definitely still in that weird limbo, not together, not completely apart—you know, our standard." Pushing myself up slowly, I lean back against the pillows, my eyes finally adjusting to the light. "I didn't tell him Pax is staying here."

"And?" Laney isn't grasping the picture, but why would she? I've never let her know the Paxton part of me, and that's the dangerous part—there is a Paxton part of me.

I continue, not directly addressing her question. "He was pissed at first, but then he did his normal thing because, let's face it, he doesn't really care."

"Cass, what's the stupid part? Last night you said you were going to do something stupid and it would be my fault. So, what is it? Is it the fact that you stay in this mess of a non-relationship?" She doesn't sound annoyed, just her usual Laney style of matter-of-fact.

"The stupid part is Paxton," I say, almost in a whisper, because if I say it out loud, it makes it mean something.

"Paxton?" Laney questions, and then a small gasp sounds through the phone. "Did something happen between you two?"

"No! I mean, not really. Oh Jesus, Laney, it isn't really like that, but it's just something…like a storm brewing. It's always… Shit, forget it." I close my eyes. "It doesn't matter because it's Pax and he'll never change. Things will never change between us."

There's a short silence, like we're letting my words settle, allowing ourselves to accept them and move on.

"Okay." Her voice sounds strange, like she's resigned to the fact that she missed some crucial part of this conversation but understands she's never going to get it again. "Well, my only advice for what I actually know about, which is this thing between you and Richard, is to figure it out and do it quickly. It's time, and it's destroying you. You make things too easy for him, and it's about time you start caring enough to put yourself first, for you to choose you and figure your shit out with him, for you and no one else. No matter who…" She trails off, either because she can't or doesn't want to finish her statement.

"You're right." I sigh. "It's going to take time. Richard and I need to talk; I owe him that much—I owe myself that much."

I can practically hear her rolling her eyes through the phone. "Whatever you say. Just do something, Cass, anything, as long as it's something. I'd prefer it be something different, but know I'm your best friend first and always, no matter what, no matter who—"

"I know. It's the one thing I've never had to question. Thanks for that Laney. I love you."

"I love you too. Try not to be stupid without me," she jokes, unable to be serious for too long.

"Bye," I say, then add, "Happy New Year, and don't think I don't plan on getting you back for this whole living situation you put me into with Paxton."

"Happy New Year! I love you, like whoa! Always will!" *Click.* She hangs up without another word. Shaking my head, I laugh out loud at her. I can never stay annoyed with her for long, and as for the Richard thing, I know she's right.

I lie back again, staring up at the ceiling.

Richard didn't stay last night. It's been more than a month since I've let him do more than kiss me. Last night, he finally brought it up, and we argued—again—then he left, saying he didn't understand but would respect my wishes. I convinced him I wasn't feeling well and had had too much champagne, and I almost convinced myself of the same thing. I haven't truly acknowledged that it's been since the moment I looked up from my birthday candles into the eyes of a ghost from my past.

Now that ghost is sleeping in a room across this small apartment from mine.

I need to talk to Paxton, set some boundaries, because my heart is beginning to forget that we don't want to let Paxton Luke in; it's the key to our survival. I also need to figure out what he was thinking last night.

Throwing the covers back, I slowly move off the bed, my head spinning a little. Damn the bubbly...or maybe it was the tequila. Both are so good going down, but so brutal the next day. Walking into the bathroom, I open a drawer, pull out some pain reliever, and then switch on the water. I cup my hand, place the pill on my tongue, and drink a bit of water to help it slide down and start working its magic.

Surprisingly, I get dressed fairly quickly and decide coffee is necessary to continue life.

Walking out into the living room, I find Paxton looking out the window, phone to his ear. I stand, watching him. He hasn't seen me yet because his back is to me. He doesn't have a shirt on, and I can see every edge of muscle across his torso and over his shoulders. His jeans are hanging low on his hips and he looks relaxed. He's beautiful in the morning light.

Suddenly, as if he can sense someone watching him, he swivels around.

Our eyes meet, a small moment passes between us, and then a shadow falls over his gaze—one that's impenetrable, one I don't think I've ever seen—but he smiles anyway. I don't like it because it's forced. I recognize it because I've used the same smile against him in the past.

He points at the phone, waves, and then turns back around.

I watch him a moment longer than head into the kitchen and pour myself a cup of coffee.

When I walk back into the living room, Paxton isn't anywhere to be seen, and his door is closed.

I need to talk to him, so I take a seat on the couch, facing his door, and wait. I finish two cups of coffee and still no Paxton. I know he's still here because I can hear him moving around his room. Resigning myself to the fact that he's not coming back out any time soon, I go get ready to meet a couple of my girlfriends for an early dinner.

Hoping he would've made a reappearance by now, I look around the apartment for any sign of Paxton; he must have snuck out while I was in my room.

I leave with an uneasy feeling. Something has shifted between us again, and it's a shift we may not be able to come back from this time.

Twenty-Four

PRESENT

Paxton

When I wake up with a slight headache from last night's shots, I can only think about one thing—Cass—and that's unacceptable. I won't be a fool. She's with Richard—hell, he's probably curled up beside her as I lie here. The thought causes a shooting pain through my skull, so I pull myself up and start my day.

My mom calls, and from what I can tell, there are no signs of Cass or her friend, no sounds coming from the living room, so I decide to venture out of my room.

I move around the apartment, listening to Mom tell me about the party the Fredricks had last night and how Dad and Mr. Porter had a few too many glasses of wine. Stopping in front of the window, I think about my own overindulgence and how I made a mistake with Cass. Sure, I've teased her with a kiss before, but this time was different. She knew it, I knew it, and neither of us can take back what almost transpired.

Now, all I can do is try to figure out a way to move forward, get past it, and still live with her. I will just need to start looking a little harder for my own place.

When I turn around to find Cass silently watching me, I freeze. *My god, she is so beautiful.* There is an awkwardness between us now. I wonder what she's thinking, but I'm not ready to ask, not ready for that conversation to happen because I need to think. I need time to think. I can tell she wants to press the subject, wants to talk now, and more than anything, I can see the hope in her eyes for everything to just be normal between us— our new normal. I just don't know if I can give that to her, so I point to the phone, smile, and turn back around as casually as I can.

I still feel her watching me and almost as soon as she goes into the kitchen, I go hide in my room, pretending I'm not hiding at all and pretending I'm not a coward.

Currently, I'm trying to keep myself busy doing completely trivial things to pass the time. I know Cass, and she's waiting for me. She decided we need to talk—I saw it in her eyes—but I'm not ready.

Pulling me from my thoughts, my phone begins vibrating on the bed next to me.

Without thinking to look at it first, I tap the talk button. "Hello," I answer, my thoughts still on this situation with Cass.

The voice on the phone is not exactly the ideal person for me to be talking to if I want to try to get my mind off the person I'm living with.

"Hello big brother." She sounds like she's up to something, and I don't like it because it means I'm most likely going to end up with a bigger headache than I already have at the moment. "Happy New Year."

"Hey, Laney." I greet her with the hope we can divert the conversation from whatever direction she hopes this is going to take. "Happy New Year. How was your night?"

"I worked." There is a bit of edge to her voice. "And yours?" she asks, quickly changing the subject.

Thinking about my night, I decide to keep my answer as simple as possible because this is Laney—she notices all, and she pounces like a lion hunting its prey until you're completely incapacitated and under her control.

"It was good, low key—went out with Matt to a bar nearby," I answer, hoping my answer will satisfy her. It doesn't.

"Hmmm, well that seems incredibly boring and uneventful, yet I got the impression from Cass that I missed something big." Her voice remains calm, but there are implications hidden behind every word. I need to think about who I'm talking to before I respond.

My answer needs to be calculated because she's looking for a weak point in my apparently vague description of my night. Do I tell her I almost kissed Cass? Do I tell her it was different this time? That is wasn't just to patronize and annoy her but something else I'm not willing to evaluate?

"Really?" Nope, that's not gonna do it. She's going to destroy me with a response like that. "I—"

"Jesus, Pax, what did you do? No wait, don't tell me." She doesn't sound particularly happy to be talking to me.

"Lane, I—" I begin to say, but again she interrupts me.

Releasing a long sigh, she says, "What is going on? Don't fuck up. This is Cass. I don't think I need to say more to you. This. Is. *Cass*. And that's all I'm going to say on the subject."

"I know." It's the only thing I can think of to say. She doesn't want me to say more anyway.

I can hear the unwilling smile on her face through her voice. "Yeah, I know you do, I just hope that's enough." We don't speak for a moment then she finally says, "Bye Pax. Love you."

"I love you too."

I let her hang up first. Her call didn't help; it only made the situation worse because everything I feel is at war. I need to get out of here. I need time to prepare for the battle.

Walking to my door, I peer out and see no sign of Cass—she must have finally given up. I quickly sneak through the living room and out the door. Avoidance is always best until you can find a way to deal, and I have no idea how I'm going to deal with this.

When I make it down to the street, I release a breath I've been holding for what seems like hours.

I walk on the sidewalk, trying to decide the best way to sneak in and out until I know what to do or until I'm over it. It shouldn't take too long. Maybe a way to get over it is a night out with Matt. It's midafternoon, but there's no reason we can't start early.

Pulling my phone from my pocket, I pull up Matt's number and tap it. "Dude, are you up for a little day drinking and some food?" Food sounds good. Drinking sounds great. Thinking doesn't seem like a very good idea at all. "Yep, meet you at the same bar as last night in twenty."

Hanging up the phone, I realize this is the only way I'm going to stop thinking. Thinking right now is dangerous, so I'm not going to do it. Instead, I'm going to drown the thoughts of Cass and me away, even if I regret it tomorrow.

Twenty-Five

PRESENT

Cass

It's been nearly two weeks since the almost kiss at midnight, the moment between Pax and me that, for once, wasn't a patronizing moment to get under my skin. It wasn't about control. It was something else, and I stopped him because it scared me—but what if I was wrong? What if it was nothing?

Since that night, we haven't spoken more than a few hellos. He's almost always gone when I wake in the morning and never comes home before I go to bed. So, when I walk in the door just after five o'clock to find him sitting at the table with his laptop, it's a surprise.

I walk farther into the room and I stop, staring at him. Unease fills my chest.

When he looks up, he has a smile on his face that I haven't seen in a while. "Hey, Cass, how was your day?" His voice sounds so calm, and the question is so normal. It doesn't at all sound like a question a person giving someone the silent treatment would ask.

Tilting my head to the side, I try to figure out his game. "Uh, good. And yours?"

"Pretty good. I got a lot of work done today, so that's always a good thing." Pax sounds nonchalant, normal, like he doesn't have a care in the world, like we haven't avoided each other for the last two weeks.

He keeps doing whatever he was doing when I walked in, as if I'm not in the room staring at him, watching him with an intense curiosity, waiting for more. He doesn't even look up.

I can't hold back any longer. "Are we really going to do this?" I'm not going to pretend everything is fine between us. I've done that for years, and I'm not going to back down this time.

Dropping his pen, Pax keeps his head down and doesn't say a word. I wait, and still nothing.

"Dammit, Paxton, look at me. Talk to me," I demand, yet he still doesn't move. It's like he's frozen in place, not even breathing. Dropping my things to the floor, I stomp over to where he's sitting and slam my hand down on the table. "Don't do this!"

Abruptly, he pushes the chair back, his eyes flashing to mine. I take a startled step backward. His gaze is hard. He has a look in his eyes I've never seen directed at me—at others maybe, but never me. He's angry, and he's fighting for control.

"I'm not doing anything," he growls. "You made it clear you don't want anything from me, so dammit, don't you dare act like this is about me." It's not only his eyes that have a hardness to them; his voice is sharp too. Gone is the friendly greeting from a moment ago, replaced by frustration.

He's not about to turn this on me; I'm not going to let him. I didn't start this, he did, and I deserve to know why.

"I did not start this, Paxton Luke, you did, and I deserve more than the silent treatment for two weeks only to come home to you acting as if we've been warm and chummy." I take a step toward him instinctively.

He laughs. He actually fucking laughs.

"Who says *chummy*?" He laughs even harder. It's like a game. Everything is always a game between us.

"Dammit, stop trying to avoid this conversation. Admit it, you've been avoiding me since New Year's Eve." I take another step in his direction, leaving less space between us.

"Fine, maybe I have been, but I'm not now," he admits, still with a hardness to his voice, a lack of emotion.

Shaking my head, I think about laughing, but I really don't feel like it. "Well, that's nice for you, but I want to talk. I want us to talk about that night. I want to explain." I keep my voice calm even though I feel like I'm about to fall off the edge of a cliff.

The hardness shows a little of itself in his eyes again. "What is there to talk about? I think you made it pretty clear how you felt that night, and I'm just trying to remember that you're Cass, my sister's best friend. Cassandra Porter, the girl next door—the girl whose parents are best friends with mine, the Cass I spent my entire youth trying to protect, the Cass who was at every holiday or vacation for most of my life, because all that means something. I'm trying to remember everything I should so I can forget the one thing I shouldn't think, the one thing that means nothing." He sounds like he's out of breath when he steps toward me. We're now toe to toe, and I realize I'm breathing hard too.

The last words to leave his mouth are my breaking point, and that old hatred washes over me like a tidal wave. It's so unexpected, although it's happened to me before, on another day, in what feels like another lifetime. "Don't you dare say that!" I shout, and without thinking, I put my hands on his chest and try to shove him with all the anger and hurt inside of me. He's too fast, too strong, and he grabs both of my wrists, holding them against his chest. I try fighting him for my freedom, but he doesn't let go. He just holds them.

Then we're back there all over again, back to when the countdown started, and we're holding each other in an intense gaze, a war between desire and fear. His head lowers, and I go up on my tiptoes. Our mouths touch lightly and we don't move; we only press our lips together in tenderness. Just when we both decide to relinquish a little control, the doorbell rings. We freeze, our bodies still united by the brief connection of our lips. The air that was once heavy around us begins to dissipate with every chime of the bell.

Then we hear his voice—the person who isn't really be-tween us, but is there still.

Pax lets go of my arms and takes a step back. The hurt and anger have returned. The doorbell rings again. "I think you better get that." He grimaces, then adds, "Never mind, I'm on my way out, so I'll be more than happy to let him in."

"Paxton, I…"

He grabs his coat and shakes his head. "No, Cass."

I don't move as I watch him walk away from me, open the door, and greet a surprised Richard, "Hey Dick, she's all yours." Paxton's voice is full of tension. I hear it, and it's like a knife to the heart.

I stare at him until the door is closed and Richard is left staring at me with a confused look on his face.

"What the hell was that all about?" Richard begins walking toward me. I shake my head a little and place a small smile on my face.

"Oh, he was annoyed at me because I…I yelled at him for forgetting to pick up more coffee and creamer. You know how I need my coffee in the morning. Anyway, I overreacted a little and was a bitch about it," I lie. Changing the subject, I ask, "What are you doing here?"

Shrugging, Richard gives me a hug and I hug him back, my mind still on Paxton. "I thought I'd stop by and see if you wanted to have dinner."

"Oh, umm, sure—sure, just let me get changed. I only just walked in the door a few minutes ago." I don't wait for a response, I just leave him in the living room while I go change my clothes.

When I close the door to my room behind me, I lean up against it, sliding to the floor with my hands over my heart. I'm afraid if I let go, all the hurt and sadness will pour out until my heart is broken beyond repair.

Twenty-Six

PRESENT

Paxton

I know this key goes into that teeny tiny hole, I just can't seem to get it to hold still. I grunt and groan with my tongue out, doing my best to concentrate. After who knows how long, I get the key into the door and open it, stumbling in.

Straightening up, I pull the key out and push the door shut.

It closes with a loud thud. "Sssssssh." I place my finger over my mouth, shushing the door so we don't wake Cass up. Surprisingly, I don't find this strange at all. Turning ungracefully, I make my way into the kitchen. *Good lord, I'm starving.* Surely there's something in here I can eat.

When I called Matt up to go out, he was only mildly concerned that I've asked him to meet for drinks three times in the last two weeks. It's just that there are too many questions I'm not sure I can answer, and I find becoming numb is the best solution at this point. It's not usually my thing because I never want to lose my inhibitions. Everyone knows I don't like being out of control. It just seems like the only thing I *can* control lately is whether I drink and numb my mind or not, and I choose the mind-numbing action any time things get too hard.

Matt told me I could stay with him when I vaguely referred to the fact that Cass and I aren't getting along very well. He basically told me he isn't surprised, and I declined to say I didn't want to let her win. He just rolled his eyes and left the offer on the table.

I don't want to stay with Matt. I want to stay where I am and make it work until she moves back into her apartment.

With my head in the fridge, I begin pulling things out to examine then decide leftover pizza is the best option.

When I turn around with a slice of pizza sticking out of my mouth and a bottle of water in hand, I find Cass standing in the doorway of the kitchen, hands on her hips, looking a little peeved.

"Why are you up so late?" My voice is muffled by the pizza hanging from my mouth. "Want some pizza?" I grin as my eyes move up her long, lean legs to her tiny heather gray sleep shorts, and they don't stop there when I realize she's wearing a matching, body-hugging tank top. Her boobs…I remember what those perfectly round globes look like without anything covering them and I instantly get hard. Drunk and hard are never a good combination.

She doesn't look amused at all. In fact, she looks like she might chop my head off at any moment. "What in the hell, Pax? Are you drunk?"

"Maybe. What's it to you?" Sarcasm drips from each word.

"Don't be an ass." Her voice sounds like music even when she's annoyed, and I try to ignore what it makes me feel.

"I wouldn't dream of it." I take another bite of my pizza slice. With a full mouth, I shoo her away. "Go back to bed and leave me alone."

"You are drunk, and you're definitely acting like a dick." She is pissed now.

Her words only make me feel worse, which in turn makes me act like an even bigger asshole.

"Fine, I'm an asshole, and you're Miss Perfect." My voice is condescending. Stumbling past Cass, I walk into the living room. "I'll go to bed so you'll stop haunting me."

She follows behind me. "You mean hounding you?"

I shake my head side to side. *Man, my head is heavy.* "Nope, I mean haunting me. You're my Cass—no, not my Cass, Dick's Cass, Laney's Cass, everyone else's Cass but mine. You just can't leave me alone. It's annoying as shit because I don't want you." I hiccup. *Great.* I hate fucking hiccups. Pointing at her, I slur, "I. Don't. Want. You."

"You're an asshole." I can hear the hurt in her tone, but I don't allow myself to feel it. "Sleep it off, Pax."

I salute her then turn for my room and stagger through my doorway before falling on the bed. I turn over on my back, thankful there's no spinning.

Without thinking, I call Laney. Let's be real, I haven't thought about one thing I've said or done within the last twenty minutes, probably longer. I haven't thought clearly since I walked into this fucking apartment and that goddamn party two months ago, so why start now?

"Laney...Laney, it's me, Paxton Luke." I start laughing because I just said my full name to my own sister. My sister knows my name, so I didn't need to say it. I laugh some more. When I get myself together, I continue to leave a message. "I didn't remember, Laney. I'm not sure why or how, but I stopped remembering who I am, who she is. I just forgot. I think I've messed up. I don't think I'll ever be able to take back wanting to kiss her, and-and I mean kiss her for real. I didn't mean the mistletoe kiss ten years ago. Nope, it's nothing like that. I don't know what its like, but I know you're going to be mad because I forgot. I forgot she's your best friend. I forgot she's Cass Porter, the next-door neighbor. I forgot."

The voicemail beeps, indicating it's ending the recording. I lay the phone down and close my eyes.

"I forgot," I say out loud to no one in particular.

My phone suddenly rings, so I tap the screen to answer it.

"Helllllo," I say into the phone.

"Pax, is everything all right?" Laney's worried voice echoes through the phone. "I accidentally erased your message before I could listen to it."

"Laney! I forgot, Laney," I shout into the phone.

"Pax, are you drunk?" Her voice loses the worried sound, and now she just sounds amused.

"Maybe. Why does everyone keep asking me that?" I turn to my side and everything spins. "Whoa." I quickly return to lying on my back.

She laughs. "Don't you have someone better to drunk dial than your little sister—who, by the way, happens to be in a time zone where it's currently three in the morning. I think you better go to sleep. Night, Pax. From now on, only call me when you're sober and after stupid o'clock in the morning when people are actually awake." She hangs up.

I drop the phone beside me.

When I close my eyes, I'm thankful for the alcohol flowing through my system and its powers to erase Cass from my mind, even if it's only for a little while.

Twenty-Seven

PRESENT

Cass

I spent most of today trying to get yesterday out of my mind. I tried working on my manuscript, but I couldn't keep my eyes open because I slept like shit. Eventually, I took a nap, because I couldn't seem to concentrate on what I needed to, let alone stay awake. Paxton was the only thing on my mind. Even as I move around the kitchen, he's all I can think about.

He was gone before I even got up this morning, so I guess we're going back to avoiding one another. Maybe it's easier. This way I can figure out what I'm feeling about my life… Richard…him. It's always frustrating because I don't have time for any of this with work piling up.

The timer on the oven sounds, so I bend over and pull the lasagna out then set it on the hot pad laid out on the marble countertop. The smell of melting cheese and oregano fills the air, and my stomach growls in approval and hunger.

"That smells amazing," a voice compliments from behind me.

When I whip around, Paxton is standing in the doorway, leaning against the doorjamb. His arms are across his chest, a sheepish grin on his face.

"Thank you," I respond, unsure if it's safe to speak after our encounter last night—not to mention, I find myself reluctant to be friendly when he's been such a jackass to me.

He unfolds his arm and steps farther into the kitchen. "Look, Cass, I'm really sorry, about yesterday and last night and New Year's and every other time I've been an ass." He smiles, and my heart opens a little. "I can't explain why I've been acting the way I have, the hot and cold, the mixed signals, whatever. Let's just forget about all that and go back to our first night here in the apartment together when we were actually getting along. Can we do that?"

It's my turn to cross my arms over my chest. I'd be lying if I said it didn't hurt a little that he wants to forget because…well, just because. I guess I can put it behind me—I've spent years burying feelings for Paxton Luke, so why should doing it now be any different? Rolling my eyes, I jab, "You're giving me whiplash."

He laughs as I turn and pull a couple of plates down. I dish out a helping for each of us.

"Did I mention this smells delicious?" He's grinning when I look over at him.

"You don't get to do that," I say, exasperated by his expectation that I'll forgive him so easily.

He takes a step closer, and he smells of a woodsy sort of freshness, clean. My heart speeds up a little.

"I don't get to do what?" he asks sincerely.

"You don't get to flash that dimple at me, say you're sorry, and expect all to be forgiven. I do want to put it behind us, but complete forgiveness will take a little time," I explain, keeping my voice steady when I feel anything but.

He puts his hand on my shoulder in a casual way, but it still sends a chill across my skin. "Whatever you need, Cass." He drops his hand.

"Thanks Pax. I may not be quite ready to forgive completely, but I must be a little bit soft tonight because I'm going to let you eat my food," I tease.

Reaching over, he takes my hand in his, squeezing it. "Letting things just work themselves out sounds like a great idea. We both have so much going on and honestly, I don't want or need complications. I can promise you one thing though, I want your friendship."

I squeeze his hand back before pulling it away and turning back to making us both a plate. "I can't believe I'm saying this, but I want your friendship, too."

"I'll grab us drinks if you take our plates to the table," he offers.

"You got a deal." I pick up the plates and carry them to the table.

A moment later, Pax joins me, drinks in hand.

We sit across from one another, and he begins telling me a story his mom told him about their New Year's Eve. We laugh at the situations our parents still find themselves in; it's like they'll never completely grow up.

As the conversation carries on, I'm more and more relaxed with Paxton and our new relationship. Maybe one day we'll think about the near kisses and high emotions, but for now, this is good.

Just as I'm about to express those exact sentiments to Pax, my phone rings. It's Richard. I debate answering it, but when Paxton sees who it is, he insists, teasing me about "Dick". *God, I wish he'd quit calling him that.*

"Hey!" My voice is high because I'm trying to hold back laughter after Pax whispered something inappropriate about our parents just as I answered.

Richard clears his throat. "Hey, what's so funny?" He sounds a bit off.

"Oh, Paxton and I are having dinner and he mentioned something about our parents…you know what, not necessary. What's happening?" I realized it wouldn't be funny to Richard at all so why bother. Also, I thought he was out of town, so I'm surprised he's calling.

"No, really, what's so funny?" he repeats, as if I never said a word.

The smile falls from my face, and Pax notices. He mouths *What's wrong?* and I shake my head.

"Seriously, Richard, it's nothing. Uh, is everything okay?" I can hear the annoyance in his voice but if I'm honest, I can't bring myself to care right now. It's like we just can't get in sync, and it's exhausting. He's obviously upset, and I'm not giving him what he wants—something he isn't used to from me.

"You tell me, Cass. Is everything okay?" His voice is harsh and condescending.

My eyebrows narrow. "Richard, hold on a minute." Holding the phone away, I let Pax know I'll be back. He gives me a look of concern, but I wave him off. I wait until I'm in my room before I respond to Richard. "Okay, I'm alone now."

He laughs. "What, you couldn't answer that question in front of *Paxton*?" His tone is sarcastic and unkind.

"Look, Richard, I'm not sure what is going on with you, but no, I couldn't. Obviously you're upset about something, and the personal aspects of our relationship are none of Paxton's business." I'm angry—one, because of his tone, and two, because he's implying something without coming out and saying it. "Now, as for your question, everything is exactly as it always has been from my viewpoint. It seems you're the one with an issue."

Richard releases a frustrated sigh. "It just seems you and I are in different worlds lately rather than just having different ideas about how we structure this relationship. I feel like you're farther away than you've ever been and Paxton is the common denominator when it comes to timing. So, I have to ask, is this coincidental, or is it more?"

When I answer, I'm not sure who I'm lying to, Richard or myself.

"Paxton has nothing to do with us, and I'll repeat that until you understand." I sit in a chair in the corner of the bedroom. "Look, I know I have been all over the place for months. It's just the two of us, we're so...so...I don't know, but I'm trying to figure out how we work now and in the future. I thought you understood." Although this *is* how we've always worked, I can admit—at least to myself—that recently I've been even more distant than normal.

"I do, but it seems like more lately, more than you're admitting." There it is. Maybe he's more intuitive to my feelings than I've given him credit for over the years. Now instead of agitated, Richard sounds resigned. "I'm sorry I'm being an ass. I know we're not really together so even if I wanted to be pissed about Paxton, I don't have the right, but Cassandra, you've been my girl for a long time. I can't think of a time I ever felt like I was sharing you with someone else."

I hear him. I know what he's saying, and he's right. I've never shown interest in anyone else in the last five years of our off-and-on relationship. He never knew there to be anyone else, and why should he have? There really wasn't, even if Paxton was always there. It was easy to maneuver around his ghost.

"Let's have dinner when you get back in a few days, okay? We can talk then, and I promise we'll figure this all out." I mean it. I want to figure this out so I can feel normal again because between fighting with him and Pax, I'm exhausted.

"Sounds like a plan. I'll be home around four on Thursday afternoon so I'll swing by at five for an early dinner."

"Perfect! I'll be ready." We both sound more cheerful, but lately, there is always an underlying threat to the comfort between us. "Bye Richard. See you when you get back."

He doesn't say anything for a minute, and I'm unsure if he hung up. Then he finally speaks. "Cassandra, again, I'm sorry I was a jackass."

"Richard, stop. I'll see you Thursday," I insist.

"Bye," he says, hanging up the phone before I respond.

Suddenly, I'm overwhelmed by a feeling that something has shifted between us, that there's something we both know we need to do. I only know I want to be fair, to myself and to him.

When I go back out to the living room, Pax is surfing channels.

"Hey, everything okay?" he asks without turning his head to look at me.

As I step around the couch and into his view, he looks up at me. "Yeah…yeah, all is good. I'm sorry I left you to clean up the mess." He watches me carefully. "Let's watch a movie. I'll grab the ice cream."

Twenty-Eight

PRESENT

Paxton

Matt signals the waitress for another round of drinks. The two girls he invited out with us are cute and flirty, and normally, the one on my left would be the exact kind of woman I would pass the time with. Normally...

These days, I do very few things I typically would.

I watch her out of the corner of my eye; she's fidgeting with her bracelet. Her auburn hair falls in perfect waves over her bare shoulders, and her skin is the color of peaches. Her eyes are green like the color of newly cut grass. She's beautiful, yet my mind compares every part of her to someone else.

Over the last week, since our talk, things have been good between Cass and me. We've had dinner several times, watched television, even worked around one another for several days. It may be the longest Cass and I have ever gone without fighting. The more time I'm with her, the more I want to be around her, which is not my typical response. *This is*, I think again as I peer

141

over to my left where the girl is sitting, laughing at something Matt is saying.

A girl, no strings, no attachments or emotions, just a simple attraction between two people.

"So, Paxton, tell me again what you do," says Hilary, the woman I'm with for the night. She smiles as she puts her cock-tail to her mouth and sucks on the tiny straw meant for stirring, not drinking out of. I smile back, partly because I know I'm not making this night very fun for her. She had an expectation about tonight, and I'm ruining it. She's making every attempt to get my attention, and no matter how hard I try, I just can't muster any interest.

Matt kicks me under the table and I grimace. I give him a look that lets him know if we weren't in polite company, I'd kick his ass.

Looking at the shining eyes of the woman next to me, I an-swer, "I'm an architect for the Bonner Company. And you? What do you do?" I make an effort to participate in the night. Why wouldn't I? Even if Cass is a constant in my mind, she's nothing more than my friend, and she has Richard. I told her we would move past whatever started between us, and this is me trying to move past it.

"Well, I'm a preschool teacher, and I teach yoga on the weekends." She grins.

We all continue our conversation throughout dinner. Matt regales them with stories of our childhood, and I even tell them about living on the east coast for years and in Europe for a year. By the end of happy hour, I can honestly say I'm having a great time. It's obvious that if I wanted to, I could continue the even-ing with the teacher at her place. Again, if I were acting like the real Paxton Luke, I wouldn't even hesitate.

Tonight is different, though; I'm different, yet I'm not par-ticularly willing to admit the reason behind my change.

Matt turns to me. "Let's hit up that new club off South Market. I'm sure the girls will be into it." He glances in the direction of the ladies' room where our dates disappeared a moment ago.

"Nah, I think I'm going to call it a night," I inform him, bracing myself for his reaction.

"What the fuck, dude? What's your problem tonight? You've been quiet all night and now this!" Matt rants. "She's hot," he adds, like I'll change my mind if he points that out.

I release a low, humorless laugh. "Yeah, I have eyes, but I don't know, dude. I'm just not feeling it tonight."

Rolling his eyes, Matt shakes his head. "You haven't been feeling it for a while now. It's not just tonight. What's going on with you?"

He waits for me to answer, and I think about what he just said. Is it true? Have I been acting differently for more than just tonight? I guess if I'm honest, I haven't completely felt like myself since arriving back home, and then there's this whole new-found friendship with Cass.

Downing the last sip of my beer, I shrug my shoulders. "I don't know, I just feel like I want a change. Maybe I don't want to keep doing the same thing over and over anymore. The only problem is, I don't know what it is I want to do differently. Maybe it's time I grow up and admit I just might want something different than what I always thought I wanted."

"You're freaking my shit out. I don't think I ever thought you'd change, or want anything different. I guess I'll call it a night too, and we can hang at my place," Matt offers, but I can hear the disappointment in his voice.

"Seriously, I just want to go home. You go out, have fun. It's not like you need me to be your wingman." I slap him on his shoulder.

"Home? Isn't Cass the Sass there? How's that going any-way?" Matt knows the history between Cass and me; he's been around as long as she has.

I rub a hand over my head and down my face. "It's fine. Cass has actually been pretty awesome, and *man* can she cook. The most interesting thing is that we're getting along." By the look on Matt's face, I can tell I'm shocking him with my answer.

Hands on his hips, he grins. "Huh. Okay, I'm not even go-ing to go there and tell you how freaky it is to hear you talk about her without sarcasm. Does this mean she doesn't hate you anymore?"

"I don't know what it means," I state solemnly. His brow quirks up, but he doesn't push it like I know he wants to. It's the best thing about Matt—he knows when to quit.

The girls are heading back toward us, new coats of lipstick on their lips and smiles on their faces. She really is hot. As they walk up, I stick my hand out in a gesture to keep things friendly and to also signal my departure. "It was so nice meeting you both, but I have to get out of here." The smile drops from Hila-ry's face. "Enjoy your night. Talk to you later Matt. Be nice to these ladies and treat them to a good time," I say as I walk away backward toward the front of the bar.

When I step outside, I take a deep breath of the cool, foggy air around me.

I can't believe I'm walking away from a beautiful girl who is most likely a sure thing to go home to watch television and go to bed alone. Matt's right—I've lost my mind.

Twenty-Nine

Cass: Age 7
Paxton: Age 9

Paxton

D ad finally replaced the wheels on my skateboard, so Matt and I are cruising around the neighborhood. Mom even said I could start riding my board to school now that I'm in the sixth grade.

"Hey Pax! Watch me jump this curb," Matt shouts as his board gains a little air on the small cement obstruction.

"Dude, that's easy. We need to find something to build a ramp with." I pick up my board and walk into the garage, looking for any materials sturdy enough to use to make a small ramp, one my mom will approve of—she's a worrier, or at least that's what my dad says.

Matt follows me into the garage just about the time Laney and Cass come running out of the house.

"Mom said you have to play with us!" Laney announces. When I look at Cass beside her, she's staring me in that weird way she does.

"Whatever! We're making a ramp, and you're a girl. You'll get hurt and then cry and I'll be blamed for it, so no way!" I shout as Matt stands beside me, nodding his head in agreement.

Laney stomps her feet and lets out a frustrated groan.

Cass smiles brighter. "I can do it. I won't get hurt. I'm good at skateboarding!"

Matt and I burst out laughing, doubling over at the waist. I catch a glimpse of Cass's face—there's a frown there now, and she looks like she might cry. Now I feel a little bit bad, but only for a second. I do hate hurting her feelings though.

Laney pushes her shoulders back and steps in front of me. "Be nice, Pax! We can do anything boys can. We'll prove it to you!"

My eyes narrow at my little sister. "Wanna bet?"

Laney narrows her eyes back at me. She may be two years younger and a couple of inches shorter, but she is tougher than most girls I know. We're standing toe to toe now and she snarls, "Absolutely!" She sticks her hand out toward me so we can shake on it. Matt and Cass stand to our sides, glaring at one another in support of their teams. "What do Cass and I get when we win?"

"I'll let you play with Matt and me for a month, no questions asked." Matt sighs next to me so I jab him with my elbow. He winces but keeps his mouth shut. "If we win then I get to have all of your bacon at breakfast for the next month."

Laney and Cass look at one another with huge grins on their faces then Laney turns and sticks out her hand. "Deal! Let's shake on it."

I take her hand and seal our agreement.

For the next thirty minutes, we build our makeshift ramp. It's not bad for two eleven-year-old boys and a couple of little girls. Since I'm the heaviest, I test it out to make sure it can support our weight.

"Okay, let's go. Matt and I go first then you two," I inform Laney and Cass. They nod their heads in agreement and sit on the curb to watch.

Matt goes first and makes a pretty impressive jump, throwing his hands in the air in triumph for effect. Laney glares at him while Cass claps. Now her eyes flash to mine, and again, I feel weird because of what I see in them when she looks at me. It's strange. Her face gets all shiny, and her eyes are full. The worst part is I think she looks kind of pretty when she does it, but...*gross*. For one, it's Cass, and two, I want nothing to do with girls.

When I come up on the ramp, I reach down and grab my board, lifting it into the air with me. Matt yells, Cass claps, and Laney just grimaces. I land smoothly and skate directly back to where the girls are sitting.

"Okay, who's first?" I ask, giving Laney a sharp look.

Despite my hinting, she doesn't stand up first, Cass does. Beaming at me as usual, she reaches for my board, practically singing her response to my question. "I am."

Reluctantly, I hand her the board. "Are you sure, Cass?"

She pats me on the shoulder like she's petting her cat and nods her head. "Yep, I'm positive. Don't worry Pax, I won't get hurt."

Putting my hands on my hips, I stare her down. I hate when she and Laney talk to me in that motherly way. "Well, if you do, don't you dare let me see you cry! Crying is for wimps!" She flinches a little when I say it and once again, the hurt I see makes me feel kind of bad.

Laney stands up and pushes my shoulder. "Shut your pie hole, Pax! Cass is brave and tough!" I just roll my eyes.

Cass walks at least five yards away from the ramp for a head start, and I can see her lips moving as she counts to herself. There's only a moment of hesitation before she's skating toward the ramp, gaining speed as she goes. Cass hits the ramp at full speed, her eyes wide as she bends to catch the edge of her board, and it's perfect. I watch in awe.

Then it happens—she lands just a little bit off balance and the board goes flying out from under her. She screams. Laney screams. I'm running toward her before she ever hits the ground. I make it to her within seconds of her landing sideways, hand out to break her fall.

So stupid. I should've never made this bet with them.

When I bend beside her, I can see her wrist is definitely broken. I say her name, but she isn't making a sound. "Cass?" I say again. Matt and Laney are standing beside us now, but I don't even pay attention to them. I wait for Cass to say or do something. Her head turns in my direction, and when her eyes meet mine, I'm amazed to find her not crying. She's only biting her bottom lip and water is shining in her eyes, but no tears fall. Not a single one.

"Laney, go get Mrs. Porter," I order without looking away from Cass. Laney runs off in the direction of the house. Cass is cradling her arm against her chest. "Cass, put your arm around my neck," I suggest gently. She does as I said, and a tiny whimper escapes her when she first moves. I slide my arms under her long, gangly legs and scoop her up.

Luckily, she isn't very heavy, so I carry her toward her house just as Mrs. Porter comes running out with worry on her face and Laney not too far behind her. Matt is scrambling at my side.

"Oh my gosh! Cassandra!" Mrs. Porter screams as she draws nearer. "Paxton, put her in the car."

Matt opens the back door so I can place her in the back seat and Laney jumps in on the other side while Mrs. Porter runs into the house to grab her keys. I've never seen her move so fast.

When looking back down at Cass's face, I see it's white as a sheet, which makes my stomach turn because normally she's the shade of caramel candy. Her eyes are wide and bloodshot, but still no tears. As I set her down, she shakes her head and holds on to my neck. She won't let go, and after a second I realize she wants me to go too. I climb in without putting her down, and it feels strange being worried about her.

It doesn't feel like the same kind of worry I felt when Laney had the chicken pox, and I heard mom say her fever was dangerously high. This concern seems different.

As we pull out of the driveway, all of us piled into the Porters' car, Cass speaks for the first time.

"Pax," Cass says weakly, and I look down at her.

"Yeah?" My throat feels a little tight because I can see the pain in her eyes.

"I didn't cry," she whispers, and then she closes her eyes.

A small smile stretches across my face, and I just look out the window, holding Cass, protecting her.

Thirty

PRESENT

Cass

When I open the door of the apartment, I can barely stand up, and my stomach is revolting against any movement.

"Cass, our reservation is for an hour from now. Why aren't you dressed?" The tone of his voice is agitated as he brushes past me. He doesn't even glance in my direction—if he had, he would have seen me stumble and put my hand against the wall for support.

"Seriously, Cassandra, we need to go or we will never make it on time."

He finally swings around, looks up from his phone, and takes me in. "What the hell is wrong with you?" He grimaces but takes a hesitant step toward me, slightly reaching his hand in the direction of my forehead then pulling back just before he makes contact.

I wrap one arm around my middle. "I don't feel very…" I can't finish my sentence because I realize I need to make a mad dash for the bathroom. I need to get to the toilet because breakfast and lunch are about to make a reappearance. Richard jumps back as I run past him with both hands covering my mouth.

I barely reach the bathroom in time. *Jesus, I want my mom right now.* I've never been very good at being sick. I feel tears beneath my eyelids, on the brink of spilling over. The stress I feel in my stomach is painful. The tile floor feels cold and clammy, or maybe that's me. Once I stop heaving, my head falls to my forearms, which I have folded over the toilet seat.

"Uh, Cassandra, are you okay?" Richard asks from the doorway. "Can…Can I get you anything?"

He hasn't ever been very comforting in situations like this. Over the years in our relationship, I've learned a few things about Richard, one of them being that he doesn't take care of sick people—not even the girl he says he has some sort of commitment to. This is huge—the fact that he's standing this close to me, even though he's still five feet away. I can't open my eyes because the thought of moving them makes me nauseous, and I can only imagine what actually moving them would feel like. I really want him to come hold me, but I know that's not an option. "A glass of water please."

I'm not sure if he answered me or not. I don't think I even register him leaving or coming back until I hear the clanking of the glass being placed down on the tile floor beside me. "Cassandra, I left a glass of water beside you…I'm going to go…I'm sorry, but I can't get sick right now. There's too much going on at work," Richard mumbles from the doorway again.

I want to call him a fucking prick. I want to ask him if he's fucking kidding, but instead, a low moan is all that leaves my mouth. "I'll check on you later," he tells me just before I hear his footsteps retreat from the bathroom and then the distant sound of the front door closing.

God only knows how much time passes before I open my eyes again. I'm only aware that I have emptied myself of what seems like two weeks' worth of meals. I'm cold, and perspiration glistens across my skin. I'm lying on my side with my cheek to the floor, and everything hurts. My top is soaked through, and I need to get it off. Slowly, I begin to peel my shirt up my body, succeeding at getting one arm out before it falls limply to the floor. Another agonizing moan echoes through the bathroom. *This is straight-up bullshit.* I feel like I'm dying, and the guy who has supposedly cared for me for years left me on the bathroom floor, practically helpless. I reach for my waist of my skirt and slide it clumsily down my legs until it's at my feet then gingerly kick my feet until I'm free. My shirt is still halfway on, but I can't move quite yet. My limbs weigh a hundred pounds each, and the thought brings tears to my eyes. I couldn't be any more pathetic.

Okay, maybe if I start calling for my mommy like I really want to then I may be more pathetic, but I won't. I'm a twenty-six-year-old woman whose non-boyfriend left her alone on the floor of her best friend's bathroom when she's puking her brains out... *Oh god, I'm so pitiful.* Tears begin streaming down my face, creating a tiny puddle on the tile next to where my head lies. *And now I'm crying.* These tears are exactly why I hate being sick—it makes me vulnerable, and being vulnerable makes me emotional. I'm just going to close my eyes...then maybe all of this will go away.

"Cass! What in the hell?" a voice shouts, waking me from my haze. I try to open my eyes, but it seems impossible. A cold hand touches my forehead first, then my neck, arms, and face, gently but frantically. My eyes finally open enough for me to see Paxton kneeling over me, worry etched across his features. Before I can say anything, he's lifting me into his arms, cradling me against his chest. "I've got you, Cass. I'm just going to lay you on the bed." His voice sounds soft and soothing, and the worry I hear makes me want to start crying again, though for a different reason this time. "Jesus, Cassandra, you're burning up." His lips lightly touch the skin of my forehead then Paxton carefully sets me on the soft, plush mattress. "I'm going to get a wet cloth and some water." He pauses, caressing my cheek softly, then continues, "And a trash can."

Closing my eyes, I sigh in relief because this bed feels a hell of a lot better than the cold, hard tile floor of Laney's bathroom. I don't even care that its's Paxton that's here while I'm half naked, or that if I could actually open my eyes, they'd probably be all heart-shaped just thinking about the fact that he's taking care of me. *Oh, fuck!* I can't be sick. I don't want him to see me this way—not Paxton. Anyone but Paxton.

"I'm going to sit you up." His voice startles me awake. I hadn't even realized I'd drifted back to sleep. "It's just me," he says softly. Carefully, he lifts me up so I can lean against the pillows. Paxton handles me in the most nurturing manner, and my eyes begin to sting again. I feel on the verge of death, and I can't guard my heart. *It's just me*—such a simple thing to say, but there is nothing "just" about Paxton Luke.

Lifting the glass to my lips, I do my best to take a sip. It's cool to my tongue, and I'm filled with a small sense of relief. "Thank you." It's barely a whisper. I look at him for the first time since he picked me up off the floor, and he looks so...so... so Paxton. Effortlessly good-looking. Completely unaware. Utterly oblivious to the effect his presence has on the world around him. Without hesitating, I reach for his hand. I'm definitely not thinking clearly.

I catch him glancing down at my hand covering his before he moves to pick up the wet cloth he brought for me. My hand falls to the bed.

My eyes close of their own volition and everything fades into darkness.

When I come to again, I can feel the cool, damp cloth smooth over my skin. I release a quiet, appreciative sigh. "Welcome back." I can hear the relief in his voice. "I'm going to let you get some sleep. Let's leave the washcloth around your neck to cool you." He starts to leave. My mouth is too dry to speak so instead, I reach out with every bit of energy I can muster and take hold of his wrist.

"Stay…" I croak. "Don't leave me again."

He stops and although I feel myself drifting back to sleep, I hear him say, "I won't leave you."

Pulling on his arm, I do my best to move over on the bed to make room for him. He follows my movements and lies down beside me then places the blanket at the end of the bed over me. He takes my hand in his and allows me to cradle our interlocked hands against my chest. I release a long sigh, and a hint of a smile touches my lips.

"I can't lose you again." My words are barely a whisper.

"Cass, what are you saying?" Paxton asks, sounding confused and concerned.

"Don't leave. Sleep," I say just before I drift off once again.

Thirty-One

PRESENT

Paxton

Opening my eyes, I feel a bit disoriented and unaware of my surroundings. The light streaming into the room is blinding and I shield my eyes instinctually. Suddenly, I'm alerted to the warmth of someone holding my hand and remember falling asleep with a very sick Cassandra talking nonsense. I'm not sure how long I lay here awake last night, thinking about the last words she spoke before she drifted off to sleep.

Turning on my side, I allow my gaze to roam over her soft, feminine features. The delicate way her lashes curl up when her eyes are closed. The small mole just above the corner of her mouth. Cass is arresting, captivating. My thoughts begin to overwhelm me—she overwhelms me.

"Cassandra?" A male voice startles me from my thoughts. I turn my head to find a stunned Richard standing in the doorway. I'm trying to read his expression, but it's like he can't decide how he feels about the fact that I'm lying here in bed with Cass curled up next to me, my hand in hers. A laugh bubbles in my chest. "Uh…hey Paxton," he finally says, quietly.

I better put this guy out of his misery. Gently, I remove my hand from Cass's clutch.

"Hey Dick." He scowls at my nickname for him. "We should probably let her sleep; it was a rough night." I get up and walk past him to the other side of the bed. Lightly, I place my hand against Cassandra's forehead. She no longer feels as hot as she did last night, and I sigh in relief.

When I look up, Richard is still watching me with a curious look on his face. "So, you stayed with her all night? I guess I'm glad to know she wasn't on the floor the whole time," he states, his voice still sounding annoyed.

Lifting my brow, I look at him quizzically. "You what?" I'm trying to put two and two together based on what he just said. "How'd you know Cass was on the floor?" I'm afraid I'm not going to like his answer.

"Well, I was here when she got sick, but I don't do sick very well. Work and being sick really doesn't work for me right now."

"You left her?" My face feels like it's on fire and my hand is beginning to twitch. "She was lying on the bathroom floor, vomiting and feverish, and you thought it was okay to just leave her alone?" His eyes widen as I start to take a step forward.

Before I can move too far away, a tiny hand wraps around my wrist, reminiscent of last night. "Pax…" she says in a soft, hoarse voice.

The discussion I was just about to have with our friend Dick becomes an afterthought—for now.

"Pax," she says again.

"Hey…yeah, I'm here." My voice is calm, although inside I'm fighting a battle to keep my cool. Out of the corner of my eye, I can see Richard has moved closer. His gaze is bouncing between Cassandra and me.

"I'm thirsty," she whispers. Her eyes are opening for the first time, and when her gaze lands on mine, she gives me an almost smile. Then she catches a glimpse of the other person in the room and drops my hand. "Oh, Richard. When did you get back?"

"Yeah Dick, it's so kind of you to check up on Cass this morning. I mean, your concern for her health is unbelievable, *Dick*." Anger coats my words, and I keep repeating his nickname because I know he hates it.

He glares at me, his jaw tense. I return his penetrating gaze with one of my own.

"Richard, you shouldn't have come this morning. I could still get you sick," Cassandra says, interrupting our standoff.

"Yes, Dick, she could still get you sick. Also, she has me to take care of her." I'm not letting up. This guy is a douchebag. I only thought I didn't like him before, but now I *know* I don't like him. He left Cass lying helpless on the floor because he was afraid of getting sick himself. *Dammit*, I want to kick his ass, and my jaw twitches as I clench my teeth.

Moving his attention to Cassandra, he sits on the bed and takes her hand in his, although he hesitates slightly before doing so. "I shouldn't have left you. I'm sorry." He tries hard to pretend he isn't paying attention to my continued observation of his proximity to her.

"I understand," she replies weakly. "Actually, I don't really understand, but I know you don't do sick people, so I guess what I mean to say is, I get you and your reasoning for leaving me."

An irritated huff escapes me, and they both look in my direction. Why won't she call him out and tell him he's an asshole? I stare right back at Richard without apology. He at least looks like he feels somewhat like a jackass, but then his eyes dart

to mine. I realize then that he feels bad more because I was willing to help her and it makes me look good.

Cass looks over at me, and I watch as she tries to gather her
thoughts. "Thank you, Pax, for taking care of me. I'm sorry if I
was a pain in the ass." She hesitates before continuing, "God,
I'm thirsty."

The look on her face brings a smile to mine, especially
when I notice Richard grimacing. "No problem. I'll leave you
two alone and get you more water." She nods, the smile she had
fading as a blank expression covers her face, one I can't read. I
hate when her walls go up, and it seems they're suddenly back
up. Glancing one more time in Richard's direction, I can see his
relief that I'm leaving the room. I'd like nothing better than to
stay right there if for no other reason than the fact that he wants
me gone.

I don't stop until I'm standing alone in the kitchen. Placing
Cass's glass from last night in the sink, I decide to pull out a
clean one for her.

Once I fill it up with cool tap water, I make my way back
down the hall until I'm just outside her bedroom door. Listening
to their hushed tones, I barely make out Richard apologizing
again. Cass tries to ease his mind then I hear him say my name,
and there isn't anything friendly about it.

When Cassandra responds, I can tell she is defending my
actions and hers, and frustration seeps into her voice. She sounds
so small, and it only makes me feel more protective. He left her
alone, on a cold bathroom floor, sick with fever, and *he's* giving
her a hard time.

Footsteps grow louder until I'm standing face to face with
Richard outside the doorway. His eyes are sharp, searching for
the answer to a question he hasn't even asked. My manner is un-
apologetic for eavesdropping on their conversation, and even

more unrepentant for being the one who took care of Cass when she needed someone.

"Here." I hold the glass of cool water out to him. "She needs this, and maybe take her temperature too. It was pretty high last night." My voice is cold.

Without another word, I turn on my heels and walk directly into my room, shutting the door behind me. I sit on my bed with my head in my hands, willing the unfamiliar feeling of jealousy to leave my mind…and my heart.

Thirty-Two

PRESENT

Cass

Walking through the doors of the restaurant, I glance around, searching for Richard. We're finally having the dinner date we missed the other night when I was so sick. He's kept his distance after showing up the day after I fell ill, saying he was letting me have time to get well. I wanted to roll my eyes at his explanation, but it's Richard. He's never once been overly concerned or nurturing when I've been sick in the last five years. The more I think about it, the more I think Laney is right. Richard and I have an unusual relationship.

It's worked for us. The benefits were mutual. There weren't any of the pressures that come from a normal relationship, and we cared enough about one another to respect each other. It was the deal. Every time we tried for more, it didn't feel right, so we would talk and fall back into our usual pattern. There was never anyone else, and I was okay with that because having someone else created complications.

I spot him sitting at the bar and wave when he sees me too.

"Hey," I say as I walk up to him and place a kiss on his cheek.

He smiles. "Hey back."

Taking a seat next to him, I pick up the drink menu.

"Should we order an appetizer and just sit here?" I ask without looking up at him, continuing to skim the menu.

Placing his hand over mine, Richard sighs my name. "Cassandra." I hear a quiver in his voice, like saying my name caused him pain.

Lifting my eyes to regard him, I examine his face. "What is it?"

A sad smile forms on his features. "You know. This is really your conversation anyway."

Swiveling in my chair to face him, I raise my eyebrow in question. "Oh? *My* conversation? That's strange, because I don't recall having a conversation planned for tonight other than the typical back-and-forth banter between two people in an intimate relationship."

His smile disappears. "Oh come on, Cassandra. It's been coming for months now." He takes a drink of his whiskey on the rocks. "We agreed from the beginning to always be honest."

"And I've never been anything but honest."

"Really? Because I feel like lately, you're lying to both of us, especially to yourself." His tone is accusing, and I don't like it.

I can feel my face flushing red. "What in the hell is that supposed to mean?"

"It means this"—he waves his hand between us—"doesn't work for you anymore."

"Did you really just speak for me? Maybe it's that this relationship doesn't work for *you* anymore and you're projecting." My words are quiet, but my tone is loud.

"Cassandra, I'll be honest, it isn't working for me anymore, but you need to be honest too." He gently takes my hand. "You have been skirting around what we're doing for months. You want more, and I'm not sure I do. I could keep doing this, but you can't, not to mention…Paxton."

I was hearing what he was saying until he mentioned Paxton—then he lost me.

"Paxton?" I blow out a breath. "Dammit, Richard. I told you there is nothing going on!" My head is starting to hurt because I'm gritting my teeth. My irritation level has never been this high with him.

"You can say it as much as you want, but there's something there. Be honest. Shit, you got distant the moment he walked into your birthday party, and it's progressively gotten worse. Then you got sick, and he took care of you, not me."

"That's your fault!" I interrupted him. "Not mine. I can't believe you're going to blame that on me! I'm the one who should be pissed, but no—no, I understood."

"You didn't let me finish. When I walked into your room the next morning to him sleeping beside you, I knew. I will always love you, but let's be real, you and I as a couple is just comfortable for us. We aren't together for any other reason, and we've let this whole semi-committed relationship go on for too long."

I look down at our hands. Mine is in his, and I feel nothing. There are no butterflies, and there isn't any real sadness. If I allow myself to be honest, really, I almost feel relief. He's right, I want more, and the reality is I've known the more I want is not with him. I've been holding on to the dependability of us because I'm scared of what I want and the possibility of it not working out.

"God, you're right." I look up at him with tears in my eyes. A lone tear falls. "I'm sorry. I'm so so sorry. I-I wasn't trying to be dishonest. I think I've hung on to us for all the wrong reasons." I take a deep breath.

"Cassandra, I didn't think you were, and honestly, we've both stayed in this for the wrong reasons. I can admit, I've been selfish. Our agreement for this crazy relationship is every guy's fantasy—no real strings, no questions asked, but faithfulness from a girl who's beautiful and kind, a girl you love. I do, you know—love you—but if I really loved you the way you deserve, I would've asked you to marry me already." Richard lifts my hand and touches his lips to my palm. It's the most intimate we've been in weeks.

"Don't apologize, you've been good to me. I didn't ask for more because I knew there wasn't really the forever kind of love between us. I'm just finally allowing myself to recognize how I've felt for a long time."

He reaches for me, embracing me with care and a respectful kind of love.

We sit and hold one another. Neither of us cares what anyone around us may think. Richard and I respect our unusual relationship. Pulling away, he kisses me lightly on my cheek before throwing back his whiskey and standing to leave. I watch him and think of the sweet moments, the hard moments, and all of the times I knew deep down this didn't work for me.

Leaning down, he whispers in my ear, "Be happy, Cassandra." Then Richard walks away.

I don't know how long I sit there after he leaves, but I sip my wine until there isn't a drop left. Standing, I walk slowly, all the way back to the apartment. The walk home is a blur.

When I reach the door, I dig through my purse, suddenly realizing I left my key on the bar. I don't feel like knocking or moving or even attempting to call Paxton, so I slide down to the floor with my back against the door and I cry. I cry for the last five years, and then I sob for all the years I spent hating someone because it was so much easier than the alternative.

Thirty-Three

PRESENT

Paxton

When I walk up to the front door, Cass is sitting on the floor, leaning against the door. She doesn't even look up when I'm standing directly in front of her.

"He's a fucking dull loser. You do realize that, right?" I squat at her feet, pushing the loose hairs hanging in her eyes behind her ears. When she finally focuses on me, I can see a lot of hurt and confusion. I reach my hand out to her, and she takes it. "Come on, Porter. Let's go inside."

Neither of us lets go of the other's hand, not even when I unlock the door and we walk inside. Instead, I lead her directly to the sofa. She takes a seat, and I sit on the coffee table in front of her.

"Look at me, Cass." She lifts her gaze to mine. "I'm going to repeat what I said a moment ago: he's dull, a nobody. Do you really want to waste any more time on that mediocre douche-bag?"

"Fuck you!" Her eyes start to blaze, but it fizzles out quickly. I don't know where that reaction came from, and I'm having a hard time deciphering if it's meant for Richard or me. Either way, it reminds me of our relationship growing up. I always did or said something, trying to protect or defend her, and *bam*, she would bite my head off.

"What happened to you?" I ask her seriously.

Eyes wide, she stares at me incredulously. "What do you mean? Nothing happened to me. Don't say those things about Richard. He really was fantastic." She focuses her attention on everything else in the room but me.

Squeezing her hand so I can get her to look at me again, I wait until she does before I say anything. "Don't get mad, but it means you used to have better taste. Cass, sure you fell in and out of love with every boy, but you always stayed true to yourself. You never settled. Hell, you always put me in my place without apology. He wasn't for you. You deserve more. The Cassandra I know would never put up with this shit from anyone. Did you really want a relationship with no real commitment? It just doesn't fit."

"You don't understand," Cass states plainly.

She stands and begins pacing the room.

Cass stops in front of the bay window looking out over the city, and it's reminiscent of my first night back in town. She stood in front of this same window with her back to me, just as she is now. I'm struck with the same feeling of protectiveness for her...and it's almost possessive. If I'm honest, it's something I've always felt when it comes to Cass. I don't move. I remain sitting, watching her and waiting, waiting for her to say something, because it's Cass and I know she always has something to say.

"It's been five years, Paxton. Five." Her voice sounds deflated, almost distant.

Standing, I walk over to her, leaving very little space between us. "I know." I take her hand in mine and them hanging between us without looking at her. She doesn't look at me either. "I know it has to be hard to walk away from him, but dammit, Cass, you deserve better than a back-and-forth relationship with a guy who smiles and is polite when he wants to be, but who we both know is manipulating you to be someone you're not!" My voice begins to rise. Turning to face her, I see her eyes are glistening with unshed tears. "Cass, you—"

"I didn't."

"Stop talking. Let me say this. No more excuses." I speak forcefully, and she flinches. "Cass, you are spirit and fire and boldness. You're beautiful when you're annoyed and breathtaking when you're kind. I know it's hard to walk away from someone you've loved for five years, but dammit, the Cass I know could do it because she is confident enough to stand up and say she's a better person without this guy." I'm breathing hard when I finish, as if I didn't take a single breath in between words.

"You're right," she murmurs, her eyes never leaving mine.

"Huh? I am?" I'm not sure those words have ever left that gorgeous mouth of hers in reference to me.

"Well, at least about the person I am, but…I wasn't talking about Richard," she clarifies. "I meant you. It has been almost ten years since you left."

Wait, what? Me? What about me?

"Me? What do I have to do with any of this?" Shock is apparent in my voice. "How did we go from talking about Dick to a conversation about me?"

"Because it's always about you," she declares, her cheeks flaming red, the tears still hanging on the edges of her lids.

"It is?" I ask dubiously. Taking a step forward, I stare hard into her eyes, trying to understand.

"I've always..."

"You've always?" I question.

"It's the way you've acted since you've been back, and when we were growing up—antagonizing me, pushing me until I'm crazy with ...with...until I'm acting irrationally and trying to beat you at your game." Cass's voice is shaking now.

"You said it's been almost ten years like you meant something more," I interject.

"I didn't!" She suddenly throws her hands in the air in frustration and begins pacing again. "I just meant you've always done this to me and...and it's basically been ten years since I saw you last. We're ten years older and yet you're still doing it. You're still barging into my life like you have a right, messing with my mind, pulling me in with near kisses and unexplainable attraction."

I don't know why or how our conversation made this turn. Is she right? Have I always done what she is saying? *Dammit*, she is right. I've always pushed things with her because it always felt like she was pulling me with a string I couldn't even see, pulling me to her, teasing me with something I didn't want but in some strange way longed for.

Without thinking, I walk up behind her, wrap my arms around her, and hold her against me.

"Cass..." There are so many emotions clouding my mind. I turn her to face me, and she abides willingly. When I look into her gaze, there are so many unspoken words there, and I can't decipher them all.

She opens her mouth slowly and whispers, "I hate you."

It's obvious she can't hold her emotions back any longer, and the tears slipping down her cheeks contradict the hate I see in her gaze. Placing my hands on either side of her face, I rub my thumbs across her skin to wipe them away. I can't take the tears, especially hers.

"Dammit, Cass, stop hating me." My voice comes out huskier than I intend as I slide my thumb gently across her plump red lips, caressing them. She shivers involuntarily. "Just stop hating me," I beg.

"I can't." She breathes deeply as another lone tear slips from her eyelid.

Moving closer to her, my body takes over and my gaze drops to her mouth. "You can," I tell her with quiet force. Her head moves from side to side in disagreement as her hands come up, wrapping around my wrists. "You can, Cass," I insist. She shakes her head again, filling me with frustration. "Tell me why then. Let me make things right between us, please." Desperation—that's new, too, like the jealousy. *What is she doing to me?*

Her grip tightens around on my arm. I look into her eyes, and there is a new sort of determination as she finds her voice and vows, "I'll never stop hating you," just before she pulls me closer and presses her warm lips against mine. Although she has taken me off guard, my body doesn't need time to react. Touching her is instinctual, like it's the key to my survival. My arms wrap around her tightly as I deepen the kiss, and she releases a satisfied sigh as if she's finally allowing herself something she's been deprived of for years. I feel it too. *Finally.*

"Cass." Her name slips into our kiss.

Abruptly pulling back, she looks into my eyes. "Shut up Pax…just shut up. We aren't talking about this because this means nothing. Words are only needed when it means something. All this is about is satisfying a curiosity so we can both move on from this push and pull we've been doing for years, got it?" She doesn't blink, and I only care about one thing: fulfilling the need to be inside her.

A slow grin spreads across my face. "Got it," I concur, sweeping her up into my arms and carrying her to my bedroom. Cass wraps her arms around my neck, locking her lips to mine in a passionate kiss.

We reach the edge of the bed, and I slowly set her down without taking my mouth from hers. Kissing Cass feels so fucking good, I'm afraid I won't ever be able to stop. Her hands move under my t-shirt, gliding over my stomach and up my chest, the sensation sending chills all over my body. When she moves them back down, Cass catches the hem of my shirt, lifting it up until I raise both arms, breaking our kiss only to pull it over my head. As soon as it's off, we both begin pulling at the other's clothes until we're both standing in front of one another completely devoid of all clothing other than her panties. My gaze roams over every part of her—the ideal roundness of her breasts, the soft curves of her hips, her long, lean legs. Her sun-kissed skin is calling for me to caress it. Cassandra Porter is my kind of perfection. We allow ourselves to take in the other completely before either of us attempts to move again.

"Nothing," she whispers when our gazes lock.

"Nothing," I repeat just as quietly. I would say anything she wanted me to in this moment.

Without hesitation, I push her back onto the bed. I lift one of her legs, kissing the side of her foot before moving my lips to the inside of her ankle and up her leg. She moans with each brush of my lips to her skin. When I reach her warm center, I run my tongue over the silk of her panties, enticing my name from her lips as she reaches out, her fingers taking hold of my hair to urge me on. My entire body is filled with so much desire, I might explode. I want release, I need it, and it takes every bit of will I have to keep it at bay. I bite the edge of the fabric, moving it aside with my teeth so I can be closer, feel more of Cass. She whimpers when my hot breath flutters across her most sensitive area. Every sound she makes gets me harder.

My tongue darts out, swiping across her wet center before I cover it completely with my lips, sucking and devouring it with my mouth, inspiring my name to come louder and faster from her until she's practically screaming it in between moans. I move my hips and allow my body to take satisfaction from the friction I'm creating with the movement of her leg and the pleasure I'm giving her with my mouth. The need to be inside her is more than I can take and I can't wait any longer. When I pull myself away, we both moan as if in pain. Stopping is painful, but not as agonizing as waiting a moment longer to fill Cass completely. She lifts her hips as I yank her panties down her legs and off her body. I reach over and pull the side table drawer open, take out a condom, and quickly roll it on my long, hard length.

Without a moment of indecision, I'm hovering over Cass, allowing one moment of affirmation to pass between us before I swiftly push until I'm completely sheathed inside her. Both of us say the other's name in a loud sigh of relief. The feeling of being inside Cass is more than I ever imagined, and as much as we said this means nothing, the intimacy of being this close means everything.

"My god, Cass, you feel so fucking amazing," I groan as I begin to rock into her, her hips matching every thrust.

"Paxton, please," she moans. "Harder."

I give in to her demand. Our movements become more frenzied, and I want the sensation to last. I want this "nothing" with Cass to go on forever. In one quick movement, I roll us over without separating our bodies, settling Cass on top of me. She looks down in surprise.

"You're in control, Cass. Take what you want," I say huskily. She bites her bottom lip, rolling it between her teeth. It's sexy as hell. A sheen of sweat glistens across her breast and my dick twitches inside her, aching for her to move. Delicately placing one hand on my chest, she gently rubs it down my front then back up. When her hand rests at the base of my sternum, her hips begin to rock forward, slowly at first, and then she picks up her pace.

"Fuck," I grunt between clenched teeth.

With my hands cradled between her hip and thigh, I help lift her up and down on top of me until we're both out of breath and Cass is crying my name out one final time. Falling against my chest, she lays her ear where my heart is still beating erratically. I lean forward and place a breathy kiss to the top of her head, her hair damp from sweat.

Lifting herself up and looking down into my eyes, Cass's gaze is searching mine for something; I'm not sure what, but it confuses me. Generally, when a girl and I reach this moment and we look at one another, now clear of our desire and need, the girl searches for something in my eyes they might be able to wrap their hope around. They never find it. I've never been able to look at a girl I've slept with with anything other than a satisfied look of thanks afterward. Cass doesn't look like she's searching for hope though. I wonder if I could I give it to her if she were.

Even if it's not hope, Cass is still seeking an answer to a question she hasn't asked. A full minute passes before she leans forward and sets her mouth against mine, lingering without moving, then gingerly she's coaxing my mouth to surrender. I shut my eyes and pretend I gave her the answer she was looking for. Then, just as fast as the kiss began, Cass ends it.

"Good night Pax. That was…even better than I imagined it would be." She pushes herself up and starts picking her clothes up off the floor.

Sitting up, I ask, a little dismayed, "Are you serious?"

Her perfect body swivels in the doorway; her clothes cover her, and an eyebrow is quirked up on one side. "Yes, I'm serious.

It was incredible, but it can't happen again," she announces with a sort of detached look in her eyes.

Fuck, is she serious? I can't tell. The night that transpired between us means nothing more than satisfying a curiosity to her. The question now is how I feel about that surprising little fact.

Do I feel the same? Or do I want this to happen again?

Before I can even respond, she's gone. Cass and I had sex, it was unbelievable…and she left me alone immediately after.

Thirty Four

PRESENT

Cass

Walking slowly through the dark living room, I fight the urge to turn back. With every step, I consider turning around and asking him the one question I need an answer to, but with each step, I keep moving forward, afraid to move too fast and even more afraid to run away from him.

I took the chance. I looked into his eyes and begged him to see the question in mine, the one I couldn't find the strength to ask out loud. Was I kidding myself? I said it meant nothing so I have no right to have expectations, but it felt so good, so right being with Paxton.

Part of me hoped he would follow me, tell me not to go back to my room, to stay with him—only part of me though. The other half is glad he didn't stop me because it would only make it harder to walk away later.

When I reach Laney's room—my room for the last few weeks—I close the door behind me.

I drop my clothes to the floor, pull back the covers, and crawl into bed. I'm unable to hold back the tears that have been threatening to fall since I turned my back on him, and they stream slowly down my face. I'm not crying because I slept with Pax; I'm crying because I saw only confusion in his eyes when I walked away.

I close my eyes, and the tears fall until I fall asleep.

I'm not sure how long I've been asleep, but it feels like hours and no time at all when I feel someone slide into bed next to me. I know it's him because I'd recognize the woodsy spice smell of Paxton anywhere. I don't move or open my eyes, not even when his arm slides over my waist and he pulls me back into his chest.

His breath whispers against my ear. "Don't ask me to leave, Cass. Please just listen." I don't say anything. I wouldn't even if I could because having him hold me feels so good. When I don't say anything, he continues, "My god, Cass, when you just got up and left, it didn't feel right, but being with you did...does. I don't know what that means, I only know I lay there wishing you were with me still. I'm trying to respect your wishes and accept that it meant nothing, but I'm not sure I can." He kisses my neck then the top of my bare shoulder.

It feels so good, it's making it hard to think, but I know I need to say something. His heart beats against my back, and I feel the quick rhythm of it—he's nervous, and so am I. Paxton doesn't move when I turn over to face him. I can tell he's holding his breath, waiting for me to respond.

"Pax, this is scary. There are so many what-ifs between us and it scares the shit out of me. You make me crazy. I'm not sure—" He interrupts me with a brush of his lips. I'm stunned at first, but when he moves closer and we're face to face, skin to skin, my reaction is automatic, natural.

His lips move down my neck and between kisses, he murmurs, "It's scary for me too. I don't know what any of this really means, I only know I want you. What happened between us didn't satisfy a curiosity, it only made it worse." Pax's lips cover mine again and he deepens the kiss. I willingly accept it, so perfect, so gentle. Every touch makes me feel alive.

His hands begin to move over my body, over my hips, until they slide between my legs. I open willingly, allowing them access to the spot they were searching for. He teases me with his fingers to give him more access and a moan slips from my lips. "Fuck, Cass, you're so wet," he murmurs as his fingers slide in, finding the spot and making it impossible to have a coherent thought. His name sounds like a demand when it leaves my mouth, a demand he willingly fulfills as he moves faster at my most sensitive spot. My fingernails dig into his back as I pull him closer, wanting him closer, needing him closer. Then, suddenly, I'm falling apart, panting his name over and over. It's like his name is the only word I know.

At the same time, with his face buried between my neck and shoulder, he repeats my name. "Cass...Cass...Cass, that's it baby, let go." His voice is reverent. I clutch him to my shaking body, and we both hold on to one another.

When I start to move my hand down his body, taking his hard length into my palm, he sighs. I begin moving my loose grip along his shaft, listening for cues from him to be sure it feels good to him. It feels almost as good pleasing him as it was being pleased.

"Faster, Cass...I'm so close," he groans. I slide my hand faster as I press my lips to his, kissing him deeply, loving the feeling of connection. I don't stop until he shouts my name one last time. "Cassandra!"

It's only a moment before he pulls me back against his chest once more and kisses my forehead softly.

"What is this?" he asks out loud. I'm not sure he expects an answer, and I can't give him one even if he does. We don't say anything else, just hold each other until we both fall asleep.

The next morning when I wake up, Paxton is no longer beside me. I feel a little deflated, but I knew this would happen. It's the reason I said all of this meant nothing. Pushing the comforter aside, I slowly get out of bed and pull on my robe from where it's lying across the chair in the corner.

Padding across the floor, I go in the bathroom to wash my face and brush my teeth. I think about showering, but decide I need coffee first. As I walk into the kitchen, I'm trying to figure out how I'm going to act around Paxton after all that happened between us last night. I come to a dead stop when the very person I'm thinking about turns around with a huge grin on his face.

"Good morning," he says, walking over to me and placing a light kiss on my lips. "How'd you sleep?" He turns, picks up a coffee cup, and places it in my hand.

Still stunned, I manage to answer him. "Umm, good. Better than good."

"Me too," he admits, placing another kiss on my lips. "Sorry, I told you I didn't think I'd be able to get enough." His smile widens. He looks happy.

A loud, boisterous laugh erupts from me.

"What is so funny?" he asks, taking a sip of his coffee and smacking me on the ass as he walks past me. "Are you naked under there?" he asks before I have time to answer his other question.

"Nothing is funny, it's just..." I begin to tell him this all feels so surreal, but change my mind. "Yes...maybe I am naked." I take in his body. He's only wearing boxers, and the V of his torso sends chills along my skin. Why does he have to be so damn good-looking?

He sets his mug down, takes mine, and places it on the counter next to his before wrapping his arm around my waist and pulling me against him. When I look into his eyes, I notice they're shining in a way I've never seen. I barely have time to notice though because he's covering my mouth with his, teasing my lips apart so he can deepen the kiss. Will I ever want to kiss anyone else?

The kiss is hard but brief. When he pulls away, he looks at me. "Damn, I wish I didn't have to leave for a meeting at the building site." His voice sounds a bit husky and full of regret. He gives me another quick kiss on the lips. "I have to get going, see you later tonight?"

I stare at him, dumbfounded. What is happening? I realize he asked me a question and I haven't said anything. "Uh...yeah, yeah. I'll see you tonight."

With one last grin, he disappears into his room, leaving me standing in the kitchen alone, confused, and a little worried that we didn't really resolve anything last night. It feels too fast—or maybe I'm thinking too much.

It's Paxton. This is what I've always wanted, or at least close to what I've always wanted...I think. Really, I'm not even sure what this is.

I realize my heart is beating fast, as it always has when I think about Paxton. This time I just don't know if I should remind it that he isn't ours.

Thirty-Five

PRESENT

Paxton

I've done nothing but think of Cass all day, even when I needed to concentrate on the detailed issues with our schedule for the completion of the job. She has taken over every part of my mind. It's everything I always knew I would feel, but never allowed myself to give in to—with good reason. I knew she would consume me. When my boss called from New York with the news of a new offer and praise for my work, I felt excited, but only briefly. It's the one thing I've worked my whole life for, and I should be more thrilled with this new prospect than I am. This is why I never allowed myself to go here, but now it's too late.

Shockingly, I told him I would need to get back to him. He was just as surprised as I am with my need for time. He gave me one day because he needs an answer. I need to see Cass.

So, when I walk in the door, I'm not surprised that my first instinct is to search her out.

I can hear the television is on. It's late, almost ten o'clock. I expected to be home earlier, but I didn't have any choice but to stay and work out every kink with this project because it's my responsibility. It's huge and means everything for what I've been working so hard to achieve.

When I walk around the corner of the foyer into the living room, I see her immediately.

She's lying on the couch in a t-shirt that barely covers the tops of her thighs. Her lacy lavender panties hug her butt cheeks, peeking just below the hem of the shirt. She's breathtaking, always has been, and it's strange standing here watching her, knowing I can touch her if I want to without question. Cass— I've touched her, been inside her. *She's mine.* The thought is something I've always felt toward her, but is it any truer now? Is she mine? Can she be? Do I want her to be only mine?

I walk to her side and she doesn't wake up. I begin undressing right there in the living room until I'm down to nothing. It's presumptuous, but I can't bring myself to even contemplate her turning me away.

Kneeling beside her, I place my lips to her ear and whisper, "Cass...wake up." When she begins to stir, I pull back and look down at her face. Her eyes flutter open and a small smile forms on her lips. I press my lips against hers gently then pull back. "Cass, I want you."

Her eyes tell me everything I need to know. I begin to pull her t-shirt up her body and she helps me. Sitting up, she pulls it the rest of the way off.

When she finally gets a good look at me, her eyes widen, and she looks at me with a quirk of an eyebrow when she realizes I'm naked.

"I said I want you," I say breathlessly as I look at her sitting naked except for her panties, her pert breasts begging me to put my mouth on them. I lean forward, taking her nipple into my mouth. She moans as I suck and run my tongue over it then whimpers when I pull back.

Rising to my feet, I pull her up too. "Is this okay?" I ask, looking into her eyes.

She smiles, and it's the most beautiful smile I've ever seen. "I want you too, Pax."

It's all I need to hear before I pull her to me, kissing her mouth hard and fast. She pushes back with as much fervor as I do. Our hands move over one another's bodies like we need to feel every part of each other to be sure this is real.

When we finally come up for air, I'm harder than I've ever been before. I place my lips against her skin as I move down her body until I can reach inside my jean pocket and pull out the one thing keeping me from taking her right now. I slip it over my rock-hard length while my fingers caress her wet center.

Standing back up, I turn her and sit on the couch, guiding Cass to straddle me. She moves over me, pressing her lips to my chest, and I sigh at the sensation it sends through my body. Her tongue darts out, and this time she sucks my nipple between her lips. I suck in a breath, the feeling shocking.

Pulling away, her eyes meet mine. "I thought about you all day." She exhales then lowers her body onto mine. We both gasp as we become fully connected, our eyes closed.

When I open mine, Cass is watching me as she begins to move up and down, creating the perfect friction. I begin moving with her, lifting her as she comes down on me.

"Fuck...Cass, you feel so damn good." My voice is a little strangled.

"Paxton," she says between pants.

We're both getting closer as we move faster until we go over the edge and crumple against one another. Our breathing is heavy from exertion, our hot bodies sticking together. Her weight feels perfect against me, and the fact that I'm still inside her makes this all feel more intimate. When she starts to move off of me, I almost stop her, but I don't. I just help her, pulling the condom off and dropping it on my clothes then lying on my side, pulling her with me in my embrace.

"Pax, what are we doing? Is this safe?" she asks me, confusing me with her question.

"Honestly, I don't know, Cass," I admit honestly. She stiffens a little. I can't tell her yet because I don't even know what I'm doing. It will hurt her, so I go with the truth of this moment. "I do know that you feel like home, and home is safe, so as long as this feels like home, I think we're safe." She relaxes.

"Home," she states simply. We're both quiet a minute then she reminds me, "You know, my apartment will be ready tomorrow. I'll be moving back home." She's only going to be one floor away, so why does that feel like too far away?

"No, I forgot. I can't believe it's been a month already. I guess Laney will be coming home soon anyway." I don't want the happy feeling of having Cass in my arms to end, but I can feel it dissipating with every word I don't say of the words I need to say.

I can feel her frown against me. "Uh, yeah, and we'll only be one floor apart. It's not like we'll be in different countries." My heart aches. She lifts up on her elbow, looking down at me. "Pax, is Laney going to be okay with this?"

"Laney doesn't have a say in what happens between us, only we do." *Jesus, Paxton keep talking. Tell her.* I just don't know what to say when I don't even know what I'm doing, what this means for whatever we just started. "Cass, I…I…"

"Stop. Don't say anything. We don't need to define this because it's home. It's safe." She lays her head back down on my chest, and I wonder if she can feel my heart being torn in two.

Thirty-Six

PAST

Cass: Age 21
Paxton: Age 23

Cass

"**C**an you believe he's still not coming home?" Laney rolls her eyes as she paints her toenails a bright shade of pink. She just returned from Paxton's graduation from NYU. I didn't go; I made an excuse of having summer classes and no time. It's been five years since I last saw him. I've only spoken to him once, on New Year's a couple of years ago. It's like he never existed, except he did, and if I'm honest, I never stopped thinking of him.

"Not at all," I say, trying to sound nonchalant.

"Nope." She uses a piece of cotton to wipe away a little polish she got on the side of her toe. "He's going straight to London. He'll be there a year, and then who knows where he will go after. What a butthole. I mean, I hate to admit it, but I miss him and was hoping he would come home."

He's not coming home, and maybe it's for the best. Maybe I can finally commit to Richard fully; I'm not sure what's been holding me back anyway.

"Well, good for him. It's what he always wanted. Pax has always wanted to work for a big architecture company and be at the top. This opportunity will get him there." I'm not sure who I'm trying to convince, but I know it's the truth.

She looks up at me. "Yeah, you're right. Who am I to try to hold him back from his dream?" She resumes painting her toes.

"Exactly. Who would try to keep him from his dream?"

I lie back on my bed, willing away the ache in my chest.

Thirty-Seven

PRESENT

Cass

It's been nearly twenty-four hours since I moved all of my things back up to my apartment, and it feels strange being in here. It doesn't even really feel like home anymore.

I'm not sure if Pax is home yet from his meeting, but I walk down the stairwell to Laney's apartment.

Instead of knocking, I use my key to go in because if he's not home, I'm just going to wait for him, but when I enter, I hear him talking in the living room. He sounds nervous and a little upset.

I walk quietly through the foyer, stopping at the edge of the living room.

He doesn't hear or see me because his back is to me; he's on the phone and he's pacing in front of the window.

"Mitch, I know you gave me an extra day, but I need more time to consider your offer," he says into the phone. He sounds upset so I remain quiet. "Of course, it's exactly what I always

185

wanted, I just thought I had a few more years." An uneasy feeling settles in my stomach. What is he talking about? I should let him know I'm here, but I remain quiet. Paxton pauses then says, "I only just moved home, I…some things…yes, I understand you need an answer. Yes…Yes…No, of course not. When do I need to leave?"

I don't mean to do it, but my hand flies to my mouth and a loud gasp slips past my lips.

Paxton swivels around, his eyes widening when he sees me. He starts to walk toward me. "Cass…"

Dropping my hand, I take a step back. I feel like I might throw up when the question leaves me. "You're leaving again?" I take a step back and turn for the door. I need to get out of here.

Paxton matches every step of my retreat and I hear him say, "Mitch, I need to call you back." As I pull the door open, his voice is almost right behind me. "Cass, please wait. Let me explain."

I run out the door, slamming it behind me. I don't wait for his explanation. I only know I need to get away from him. How could I do this to myself? How could I let him in again?

"Cass!" I hear him shout as I run up the stairway—he's just behind me.

When I enter my apartment, I shut the door, locking it behind me and sliding to the floor. That's when the dam breaks and the tears flow. I wrap my arms around myself, trying desperately to hold myself together.

A moment later, Paxton tries opening the door, and when he realizes it's locked, he begins banging on it. "Cass, please let me in!"

"Go away, Paxton. Please just go away," I beg through my tears.

"Let me explain. It's not exactly what you think. I was going to tell you tonight, was going to talk to you," he pleads with me.

"Go away, please," I cry, a tiny sob escaping.

"Jesus, Cass." I hear him slide down to the floor on the opposite side of the door, and his voice sounds closer when he speaks again. "Please, let's talk about this. They offered for me to head the office in London." His confession pierces my heart; it's exactly what I thought.

Through tears, I ask, "When did they offer you this job, Pax? Before or after?"

"God, what does it matter?" he asks, desperation clear in his voice.

"It matters," I say plainly.

"After our first night and before our second. I asked them for time to think. I wanted to talk to you about it, but when I came home and saw you lying on the couch, I just wanted another moment without big decisions between us. I wanted to enjoy just being with you. I wanted…I want you so badly. I've wanted you for years, and I finally gave in to my attraction to you. I just wanted it without being pulled in a different direction, even if it was just for one night. I planned on talking to you tonight."

I hiccup, putting my face in my hands. After a moment, Pax says my name. "Cass?"

Standing up, I open the door. Paxton jumps up and rushes me, pulling me into his arms, but I don't hug him back. When he pulls back, he looks at me questioningly and says my name again. "Cassandra?"

Shaking my head, I pull away. "It's your dream." More tears quietly stream down my face.

He reaches out for my hands, taking them as he tries pulling me toward him. "So are you. In some strange way, you always have been." His confession sparks a little hope, but the reality of our current situation and our past doesn't allow it to become a flame.

"No, you were always mine." My confession is real and raw. It hurts because I know I'm not going to let him give up this job for me, and he'll be thankful that I don't ask him to. "Take the job, Pax. It's what you always wanted, and I can't let you resent me for making you choose."

"God, Cass, no," he chokes out, tears forming in his eyes.

"I want you to leave—please leave," I ask him, almost begging. He shakes his head no, denying my request. "Leave!" I shout, pushing him toward the door.

His shoulders fall when he realizes he isn't going to convince me. Turning for the door, he only looks back when he goes to close the door behind him. He looks like he might say something, but then starts to shut the door. He stops just before it's closed and whispers through the crack, just loud enough for me to hear him, "You felt like home, Cass." Then he's gone.

A sob escapes and I stare at the closed door, trying to remember how to hate Paxton Luke instead of loving him.

Thirty-Eight

Paxton

It's been a week. I haven't seen Cass, and she hasn't returned any of my calls. I've called her at least a dozen times. Now I have exactly two hours before I have to be at the airport.

In the last week while I prepared for this move, I haven't stopped thinking about her. Even when I broke the news to my parents, the pain of that was nothing compared to the hurt of that day with Cass. She looked broken, just like the day I told her I could never love her all those years ago.

Love her…

Jesus, I need to talk to her. I drop the shirt I was about to place in my suitcase and run for the door. *Please let her be home.*

When I pull the door open, I nearly slam into the one person I want to see but least expected to. Her hand is in midair, preparing to knock on the door. "Cass!" I say in surprise.

She pulls her hand back and tucks a piece of hair behind her ear. "Oh, are you leaving already? Your mom said you didn't need to be—"

I reach out and pull her against me without letting her finish. "Cass, I…I need to tell you—"

"No Pax, I need to tell you…I'm sorry I've pushed away this last week. God, I've pushed you away practically our whole lives. I'm sorry. It's just…I can't forget you, as much as I try or as much as I should, because I know you can never pick me. I shouldn't expect you to because if I love you the way I say I do, then I should want you to have everything you ever dreamed of—"

"You love me?"

She looks at me wide-eyed, nervous, like she didn't even realize she said it.

"Cass, I can't go." Shaking my head, I hug her then push her back again. "I can't leave you because I realize now, that dream—the idea of success and everything I've always wanted from life—includes you." I let her go and begin pacing. "Shit, I almost fucked up *again*." I turn and face her, and she's staring at me with a hesitant smile on her face. "I spent my whole life chasing after something that would never be complete because you weren't there. Don't you see? It's the reason why the moment Mitch asked me, I didn't give him an immediate answer. It wasn't really my dream, or at least it wasn't all of it, the most important part of it. You are." I step toward her again, taking a hold of her arms and gazing into her shocked eyes. "Cass, I've always been crazy about you, knowing the moment I had one taste, I'd be addicted, never able to get enough of you. You've always had me wasted on your love. I love you, Cass." I grab her face and press my mouth against hers. "I love you! Do you hear me? Say something!"

Cass

The three words I've waited basically my entire life for Paxton Luke to say just left his mouth, and my mind is taking too long trying to wrap around the fact that he just said I am his dream and he loves me.

He stares at me, waiting for me to respond to his confession.

"Did I say something wrong? Oh, shit, do you still hate me?" he asks, sounding like the little boy I adored my entire childhood.

Shaking my head as tears stream from my eyes, I finally say the words I've honestly felt for years. "I love you too, Pax."

He kisses me hard and fast, and when he pulls away, grinning, he says, "Now that sounds so much nicer than you hating me."

Smiling, I press my lips to his over and over again. "I never really hated you, but there's no doubt I tried. You made it practically impossible." Then I place a long, hard kiss against his willing mouth. He kisses me passionately and with so much love.

He ends our kiss and looks down at me. "Now what happens?"

My heart feels full as I grin up at him. "I think our dreams come true."

Epilogue

Cass

Staring out the window, my eyes roam over the foggy, misty streets of London. It's peaceful. Sighing, I settle a little farther into Paxton's embrace. His lips press softly against my forehead.

"Thank you," he says on an exhale, his breath fluttering against my skin.

In the year that has gone by since Paxton told me he loved me and I told him the same, he has said this many times. When he said he'd give up everything and stay with me in San Francisco, give up his dream job, I knew I couldn't let him do it. Luckily, I can work anywhere, so we packed up and moved a month later.

"You always say that, and I've told you it isn't necessary to thank me," I tell him without turning around. "It wasn't just for you. It was for us."

He turns me around in his arms, dropping his arms to circle my waist and pull me forward. His mouth covers mine in a gentle kiss and when he pulls back, he stares down into my eyes.

"*Us*. I really love us. I will never stop thanking you for making my dreams come true," he responds.

"Our dreams," I state emphatically, taking his hand and placing it over the roundness of my belly.

"Our dreams," he repeats, dropping to his knees and placing a kiss where his hand was just resting.

When he looks up at me, his eyes shimmering with unshed tears, I caress his cheek and he leans into it. It's a safe and beautiful feeling to know he loves me.

Paxton

Her hand is warm against my cheek, her touch silky soft. Everything about the life Cass and I have shared while living here in London has been full of honesty and love. It's a life I'm not sure I ever thought would be mine, especially with the girl I spent my life trying to forget.

I kiss her round belly one more time before taking her hand again and placing it next to mine on her stomach.

"Marry me." My voice cracks with emotion, and my eyes focus on her gaze as her eyes open wide with shock. "Marry me, Cass." I slide one hand over and cover hers as I pull a ring from my pocket with the other. Tears begin to slowly fall down her cheeks, and a smile spreads across her beautiful face.

She nods her head yes, and I slide the ring on her finger. She pulls on my hand and I follow her direction, standing up as she wraps her arms around my neck, tears now flowing freely as we laugh and I hold her in my arms.

"We're going to love one another, Cass. We're going to love each other for the rest of our lives."

Her lips crash against mine.

I'll never get tired of kissing her. I'll never get tired of loving her.

I can't wait to live my life drunk off her love.

Acknowledgments

To my Dave, thank you for seventeen years of being wasted on love for you. I always thought I learned to love from my parents, but I now know that isn't true. It was you. I will miss you forever and love you even longer. Our love was a beautiful novella, one I never wanted to end, filled with love, angst, and happiness. Thank you for loving Sienna and me so completely.

To Sara Ney, thank you for your love, friendship, and constant belief in me. Your advice and inspiration are incomparable.

To Christine Kattnauer, thank you for always stepping up any time I need you. I love you.

To Laurie Darter, thank you for your honesty and love.

To all of my Nerd Herd Admins-Emma Hart, Sara Ney, Rachel Schneider, ME Carter, J.D. Hollyfield, Andrea Johnston, & Andee Michelle: Thank you for lifting me up. Supporting me. Making me feel a part of the crazy book community. And, making me laugh even when I haven't had much to laugh about. You all are my heroes.

My Rickman Rebel's leaders- Shawn Garcia, Kristen Teshoney, & Tamara Estes... thank you for your support. Shawn, you keep things afloat with your daily post.

To the Rebels, thank you for showing me love and support.

To C. Marie- you saved me. You know why I'm saying this and I look forward to many more books together.

To Julie Titus, thank you for never letting me down and your friendship.

S hirl Rickman is a writer, a dreamer, and an optimist. A small-town Texas girl currently residing in the San Francisco Bay Area, Shirl adores her husband, daughter, and two crazy dogs. When she's not dreaming up new love stories, Shirl can be found reading, drinking her favorite coffee, Kona Blend with coconut milk. She loves kindness, laughing and meeting her readers.

Website link:
https://shirl-rickman-author.squarespace.com/

Facebook:
https://www.facebook.com/shirlrickmanauthor/?pnref=story

Shirl's Girls & Cody Facebook Group
https://www.facebook.com/groups/1010382209000750/

Twitter:
https://twitter.com/shirl_rickman

Instagram:
https://www.instagram.com/shirlrickmanauthor/

Other Titles by Shirl Rickman

Falling Slowly (Falling Novella Series Book 1)

Free Falling (Falling Novella Series Book 2)

Somewhere in Between

When Destinies Collide